Where the Williwaw Blows

The Aleutian Islands — World War II

Leonard Feinberg

Pilgrims' Process, Inc.
Boulder, CO

This is a work of fiction. All characters and events portrayed in this book are either products of the author's imagination or are used fictitiously.

WHERE THE WILLIWAW BLOWS
The Aleutian Islands—World War II

Copyright © 2003 by Pilgrims' Process, Inc.

All photographs, unless otherwise indicated, are from the collection of Leonard Feinberg. Photos on pp. 19, 49, 77, 179, and 189 are from the Naval Historical Center; those on pp. 125 and 195 by Louis W. Kohlhepp; and the photo on p. 153 by Robert A. Salkowski.

ISBN: 0-9710609-8-3

Library of Congress Control Number: 2002117132

Printed in the United States of America

0 9 8 7 6 5 4 3 2 1

Chapter One

When the captain telephoned about staging the Victory over Japan Day celebration on the island of Adak in the Aleutians, I was talking to Claude Nooters, quartermaster third class. At that time Nooters, a big hulking man, held the navy record for push-ups, having raised himself from the floor and then lowered himself again eight hundred and forty seven times in the presence of three official witnesses. He was very proud of this achievement and kept dragging it into the conversation without much regard for relevance. But he wasn't very bright, and he repeatedly failed the exam for quartermaster second class, and he often got into difficulties.

"Nooters," I said patiently, "how many times have I told you never to burn any papers except those in the trash basket?"

"Three times, Mr. Ward," Nooters said, counting slowly on his fingers.

"How many times did Lieutenant Dutton tell you?"

Nooters looked resentfully across the room at the slight, intense officer with the thin blond mustache. "Two times," he said.

"And how many times did Commander Pierce warn you?"

Nooters looked down and pushed out his lower lip. "Lots of times," he mumbled.

I sighed. The day before, Commander Pierce had forgotten his copy of *Newsweek* on the desk, and Nooters had put it in with the rest of the trash and burned it. The commander was furious because he had not had time to cut out the voluptuous full-page pin-up girl that appeared in every issue of the armed services edition of *Newsweek*. He was also furious because he had left the magazine out on top of his desk, where everyone could see it. Ordinarily he hid it in a large manila folder so that unexpected visitors would find him intently studying what seemed to be official documents.

The commander had grumbled to me about the inefficiency of the office force, and I was now grumbling to Nooters, when the phone rang.

"Pierce?" the captain asked.

"Lieutenant Ward speaking. Commander Pierce is out on the docks."

"Ward," the captain said, "the newspaper correspondents tell me they want to take some pictures of the V-J celebration here. There isn't a damn person celebrating, as far as I can see, but the correspondents say they need pictures, so we'll have to send some men out there to pose for them. Pick three enlisted men from your office and tell each department head in the port captain's building to send at least three men."

"Yes, sir."

The captain hung up and I said, "Nooters, I have a job for you and Warren and Mason."

Warren, the quartermaster, looked up from the letter he was writing, and Mason, the messenger, strolled over from the coffee table.

"The newspaper reporters want to get pictures of Adak on V-J Day," I told them. "Go down to the recreation building and do what the photographers tell you."

The men walked out, then Nooters shuffled back and said, "Can I go to my hut first and put on my campaign ribbons for them pictures?"

"What campaign ribbons do you have?" I asked.

"I got three," Nooters said. "Good conduct, marksmanship, and overseas service."

"Sure," I said. "Take the jeep."

After I had relayed the captain's order to the department heads in the building, I came back and stretched out in my chair, resting my feet on the bottom drawer of the desk. Having told the captain that Pierce was down at the docks, I hoped that the captain wouldn't find him up at the club. It was possible, I thought, that Pierce actually was at the docks, but it wasn't likely. I always told senior officers that Pierce was at the docks. There were twelve docks; they were large; and it would have been hard to prove that a particular individual had not been on one of them at a specified time.

It was far more likely that Pierce was still in his Quonset. He liked to take a nap after lunch. After a while Lieutenant Dutton had started taking an afternoon nap too. Dutton, having become a lieutenant one month before me, was the next senior man in the office. He timed his naps to end about ten minutes before Pierce's, and he was always at his desk, earnestly looking through dispatches, when the commander arrived.

My nap usually ended five minutes before Dutton's.

Now, on V-J Day, I took out a *New Yorker* and glanced through it. There wasn't much to do on Adak. For a long time there hadn't been much to do on Adak, but Dutton was energetically making out a schedule for the patrol craft. The naval base had three patrol ships: one was always on duty; one was at the dock ready for emergency duty; and one was in the repair yard. It didn't take much ingenuity, I thought, to make out their schedule, and it had already been made out for the month of August. But Dutton worked away ostentatiously, pulling at his little mustache and jerkily shuffling papers.

The door opened slowly and Lieutenant Thompson came in. He was a bulky, slow-moving, slow-talking engineer who had charge of the underwater defenses in Adak Bay. When he saw that the commander was not in, he sat down by my deck. He knew that I had nothing to do with underwater defenses, but he had made the long trip from the net depot and he didn't want to waste it. He began talking to me about the University of Michigan, where he had taken a degree in engineering ten years before I had enrolled in liberal arts. It had been a long time since I had seen the campus, and it was a good deal longer since Thompson had seen it, but he managed to talk about it for a long time. I daydreamed as the slow voice droned on.

Finally Thompson stated his problem. He wanted permission to use 3/4-inch hooks instead of the regulation 5/8-inch hooks on the net he was installing. He explained in detail what the advantages of the new size would be, and I listened politely and mumbled at what seemed to be appropriate moments.

Thompson was still talking when Nooters, Warren, and Mason returned. "You know, Thompson," I said, "instead of figuring out ways to put the net up, you ought to be getting ready to take it down. The war is over now."

"Oh no," Thompson said. "I haven't finished putting it up."

"But the war is over. We don't need the net any more."

Thompson frowned and stood up. "I don't care. Nobody's ordered me to stop. By the time Washington gets around to it, I'll have the whole thing installed. You just tell the commander I want to use 3/4-inch hooks."

I promised that I would and Thompson went away. Mason put the coffee pot on and the men lighted cigarettes.

"Well," I asked, "what did you do?"

"We put on a hell of show," Nooters said. "Them old reporters lined us up and made us wave our hands and cheer while they was taking pictures. They took lots of pictures."

"That damned correspondent," Mason said. "I heard him say he's writing a story about dancing in the streets of Adak. How about that? Dancing in the streets. That son-of-a-bitch."

"What are you so mad about?" Warren asked.

"I got plenty to be mad about," Mason said, mimicking Nooter's speech pattern.

"I don't get it," Nooters said. "What you going to do when you get out?"

Mason frowned. "I ain't so sure I'm gonna get out."

"I'll be goddamned," Nooters said. "You're kidding."

"I ain't kidding. The navy ain't so bad."

"You're crazy," Nooters said earnestly.

Mason scowled. "Oh yeah? This is the easiest job I ever had. My old lady gets an allotment and don't bother me. When I'm home she's always bitching about dough and drinking and every goddamn thing she can think of. I sure don't hear her bitching here."

"Yeh, here or in jail," Warren said.

"The hell with that noise," Mason said. "I figured the war would last a lot longer." He tilted his chair back and stared morosely at the ceiling. "Dancing in the streets," he muttered to himself. "That son-of-a-bitch."

When the coffee was ready, Nooters passed the cups around, then sat down. "Yes sir, I'll be home soon," he crooned, packing his corncob tidily, lighting it, and puffing contentedly.

"You be careful when you get home, Claude," Warren said. "You got eight kids already."

"That's all right," Nooters said. " I guess I know what I'm going to do when I get home."

"That's just what I mean," Warren said. "You said there's no electricity on your farm."

"That's right," Nooters agreed.

"So when it gets dark you go to bed early."

"That's right."

"That's what you got to be careful about. You got eight kids already."

Nooters looked at Warren solemnly. "It's like I told you before, Warren," he said earnestly, "I don't think it's that so much as the fooling around at lunch time."

When everyone burst out laughing he seemed genuinely surprised and slouched back into the ship-plot room. I took out the *New Yorker* again, but before I could open it the telephone rang. The captain's aide was calling to inform Commander Pierce that he was invited to a party at the captain's quarters that evening.

"We'd better find the commander," I said.

"Yes," Dutton agreed. "You go. I've got a lot of work to do. I'm figuring out a schedule for the patrol craft."

I put on my field jacket and took the jeep. On August 15, 1945, it was as warm as it ever got in the Aleutians: fifty above. The road to the officer's club had been cut out of the mountain and I went slowly around corners where the drop to the bay below was three hundred feet. A gray canopy of fog hung low over the yellow moss and the brightly colored flowers of the tundra. The weather officer had estimated that there were twelve clear days a year on Adak. This was not one of those days.

Commander Pierce was at the club, his short pudgy body perched on a stool at the bar. He had a drink in his hand and was watching a transient officer play the slot machine. I knew the officer was a transient because none of the local men played the machine until after the twentieth of the month. The mess officer had decided that the slot machine should pay at least two hundred dollars a month profit, so it was set on the first day of the month to bring in a generous percentage to the house. After the third week, when transients and visitors had unwittingly contributed the two hundred dollar minimum, the machine was reset to pay off more fairly for the rest of the month. That was when the base personnel played it.

I told the commander about the captain's invitation and Pierce ordered drinks. We had just about finished when the door opened and a tall, slender, middle-aged man with a newspaper correspondent's insignia on his coat came in. He looked around the room, smiled when he saw Pierce, and came over.

"Hello, Buttaeus," the commander said. "Won't you join us?"

"Yes, thank you," Buttaeus said.

"Do you know Lieutenant Ward?"

"No, but I've been looking for him," Buttaeus said. We shook hands, and I was startled by the sadness in his deep-set gray eyes. Buttaeus had a very narrow face, a long thin nose, thick lips, and iron-gray hair. When the steward came over, Buttaeus asked for a glass of wine and we sat down at a table.

"Are you the man who organized the fake celebration?" I asked.

Buttaeus smiled. "No. That's not my idea of legitimate news. But the other correspondents were sending pictures, so I had to take some too. It was not a very impressive exhibition."

"Why did you want to see me?" I asked.

Buttaeus drank his wine slowly. "The commander told me you were Peter Woodley's best friend."

I hesitated a moment, then took out a cigarette and lit it. "That's right."

Pierce finished his drink and stood up. "I'd better get down to the office, Jack. Why don't you stay and give Buttaeus his interview? There isn't going to be much happening for awhile."

After Pierce left, Buttaeus smiled wryly. I noticed that his eyes remained sad. "It isn't exactly an interview I want. I've heard some rumors about Woodley and I'd like to get the whole story. Not necessarily for publication."

"What do you want to know?"

"The truth," Butaeus said softly.

I frowned. "It's what reporters do with the truth that bothers me. I don't want it twisted in this case."

"Believe me," Buttaeus said, very quietly, "I will not twist it."

I looked at him carefully. "I believe you. But it's a long story, and I would just as soon not tell it here. Let's go where we can have some privacy."

Buttaeus paid for his wine; I signed for my drink; and we went out to the jeep. I drove toward the south end of the island, on a road skirting the bay. For a moment the clouds passed and the sun shimmered on the water. The wind kicked up small whitecaps on the waves.

"It's nice now," I said, "but in a couple of months the williwaw will blow again."

"The williwaw?"

"The Aleutian wind. It comes from the Artic, over the Bering Sea, and it whips up forty-foot waves and slashes at a hundred miles an hour into Quonset huts half buried in snow. Then you see men wrapped in parkas, with only their noses showing, leaning at ludicrous angles against the wind, and stumbling slowly and awkwardly through the snow."

Buttaeus looked around. "What was the island like before the war?"

"It was bare. Even the Aleuts had abandoned it. The blue fox was here, and the ptarmigan, and the bald eagle. And Japanese fishermen. Now thousands of American sailors and soldiers are killing time here."

"No marines?"

I smiled. "Yes, there are a few marines. They guard two places on the island. The ammunition dump is one of them."

"And the other?"

"The nurse's quarters."

Buttaeus smiled. "Many nurses here?"

"Just a dozen until recently, about thirty now. There's a local legend about a nurse who earned twelve thousand dollars in six months before she was shipped home."

"It's a popular legend," Buttaeus said. "I've come across it at military bases all over the world."

"Well, Adak's had three years to build up a few legends. I suppose you've heard the one about the regular navy captain who was told that a junior classmate he hated was promoted to rear admiral. He got drunk and stayed drunk the rest of the war."

"I've heard it," Buttaeus said.

I parked the jeep at the end of the road and we walked along the creek up the hill. The creek was ten feet wide and about two feet deep. Up it, against the current and the small waterfall, through eddies and little whirlpools, scooted thousands of slick dark salmon, rubbing fins in the scrambling throng, darting up the creek. Near the top, below the steep falls, they gave up, spawned, and turned to swim easily downstream among the white bodies that had spawned and died, rotting in the swirling waters as the living fish zoomed by with irresistible persistence.

In spots the salmon were so thick that they swam just below the surface, their tails leaving tiny wakes as they zigzagged among the rocks. Here and there a fish jumped out of the water, glistened for a shining moment, then flopped back with a spraying splash. Two seamen, boys in their teens, were standing in the creek, sweeping their white caps through the water, counting the fish they scooped up. They were trying to catch one of the blue trout that followed the salmon to eat their eggs, but they had not caught any yet. The boy's dog, a shaggy mongrel, jumped into the creek and terrified the fish, who scurried frantically around and excited him.

At the top of the hill we left the narrow path and walked on greenish-yellow springy tundra, among the flowers that splatter the hillside.

"These purple and green flowers are lovely," Buttaeus said. "I've rarely seen such brilliant hues."

"They are beautiful, but you notice they don't smell. That's because of the volcanic soil. There are no trees here either."

We sat down on the tundra just above the waterfall. Looking down, we could see the creek, the sailors, and their dog. Above them a B-24 appeared, and another, and six P-38s glided and capered across the sky. The wind had stopped and the water in the bay was the limpid crystal blue of an Italian lake. Then the clouds moved and dimmed the sun and the water turned gray.

There was no flat land on the island, only irregular hills and mountains. We sat on the slope of an isolated, lonely, bare world, watching clouds gather and wisps of fog hang between hills, hiding the large volcano on the next island. Thirty miles distant, it jutted out massive and sharp, emitting a steady black smoke that the wind pushed like the puffs of a giant pipe.

I pointed to the range of rugged white mountain peaks on the northern side of the island. "All summer we've been watching the snowline climb on that big mountain. It will reach the upper third of the mountain, but it won't go any higher because the fog and clouds settle below it. And in fall and winter we watch the snowline drop until it covers the mountain. Watching a snowline moving is pretty monotonous, but then everything in the Aleutians is monotonous. The fog is always here, and it snows more than half of the year, and the williwaw blows in fall and winter. A lot of people get pretty depressed here."

Again the sunlight sparkled for a brief moment on the water; a gull swooped down into the bay; and a ptarmigan flew by hurriedly. Then a heavy mass of clouds pushed in and blotted out the sun.

"Now," Buttaeus said, "the story I heard is that Woodley was miraculously saved from death. Was he?"

I looked thoughtfully at the cloudy sky. "It's hard to answer a question like that. We're not children, and it isn't that simple. Woodley was saved from death three times when he might have been expected to die. And he himself was convinced that he had been miraculously saved. But you'll have to decide for yourself."

"All right," Buttaeus said, "I'll decide for myself. Tell me the whole story. When did you first meet Woodley?"

Chapter 2

Peter Woodley and I became friends because our last names began with W. At the Navy Officers Indoctrination School men were grouped in alphabetical order, so he slept in the bunk next to mine and our schedules were identical. We got involved in a series of comic-opera episodes, and if the navy's need for men in 1942 had not been desperate, both Woodley and I might have failed to graduate, though not for the same reason.

Woodley was twenty-one years old then, a clean-cut, good-looking blond boy. Six feet tall and weighing 190 pounds, he had played football and baseball in college. He had raced motorboats for years and he loved the sea. But he didn't like to memorize the sub-divisions of the fleet and he couldn't write a letter in correct navy format. I memorized all the sub-divisions and wrote a number of perfect letters, but I had trouble reassembling revolvers and I never learned how to tie a navy knot. In the eight weeks at indoctrination school I learned to tie only one kind of knot, and that proved to be a commonplace civilian knot that roused the voluble contempt of the boatswain's mate to whom I showed it. I never did pass the knot-tying test, nor did I ever have occasion to tie any more knots during my naval career, except once when I mailed a package of souvenirs from the Aleutian Islands.

I never reassembled the revolver I had taken apart in the gunnery drill, either. It happened a long time ago and I suppose that by now someone has managed to put it together again. But I still don't believe it was an ordinary revolver, in spite of the unsympathetic remarks of the gunner's mate who was instructing us.

Woodley had a way with revolvers and tied knots nicely, but naval correspondence upset him. After the first class meeting he said to me indignantly, "How can you write a letter without using the first person?"

"By using the third person," I said.

"I can't talk about myself like that," he insisted. "It's indecent."

I laughed but he was serious. "Look at this," he said. "My assignment is to write an official letter to the Bureau, asking for change of duty, I'm not permitted to say that I am asking for it. Oh no. I have to say, 'It is requested that Ensign Peter Woodley, DV-(s), 874-139, be granted a change of duty from the battleship *Cleveland* to a crash boat.'"

"All battleships are named after states," I told him. "There isn't any battleship named *Cleveland*."

He revised his letter glumly and brooded about the principle of the third person. He spent much more time on his letters than their eventual quality merited.

Woodley and I stood our first watch together, at midnight on our third night at indoctrination school. I don't know about Woodley, but I never felt the same about the navy after that watch. Having daydreamed for weeks of heroic action on the bridge of a typhoon-tossed destroyer, I found my first duty-station, the northwest corner of the school's mess hall, something of a letdown. Woodley sat in the northeast corner. Two other officers occupied the other corners. It was a large mess hall, but it wasn't that large. It seemed to me that I could have watched it myself. Conceivably both Woodley and I might have been required. But I felt that four officers were too many.

Activity in the mess hall during the hours from midnight to four was not hectic. A few flies buzzed around the southeast corner, near the pantries. At times I heard a scratching sound, the perpetrator of which I identified, correctly, as a rat. When I glanced at the baseboards I could see cockroaches crawling.

There we sat, four sleepy men in officers' uniforms. The curriculum at indoctrination school filled every moment of a twelve-hour schedule, and we could have used the sleep we were missing. Woodley walked over with the instruction sheet for officers of the deck and showed me the list of qualities a good O.O.D. should possess—vigilance, initiative, foresight, courage, and a half dozen other virtues. "It's a good thing everybody here is a potential admiral," he said, smiling, and then pointed to an item on the sheet and read, "'A good watch officer does not indulge in idle conversation.' That word idle can be interpreted in lots of ways," Woodley said and went back to his corner. At 0015, when it was time to make the first of the required inspections of the mess hall, Woodley walked briskly, and with what he apparently thought proper military bearing, to the corner where a round-faced officer with a sandy mustache was sitting. Woodley said, "Hi."

The officer jumped up, stood at attention, and said primly, "Ensign Nolan on duty, sir."

"What the hell," Woodley said, "I'm on watch here just like you."

Nolan's eyes darted around nervously. "Yes, sir. No idle conversation on duty, sir."

Woodley walked on, after a puzzled moment, and Nolan sat down abruptly. Woodley didn't stop to say anything to the fourth officer, who was studying his instruction sheet diligently. At 0300 Ensign Nolan marched stiffly around the room, pausing to peek into corners and, once, to look suspiciously out of the window. What he saw, by the bright light of the New York moon, I don't know. He returned to his seat.

After that, at fifteen-minute intervals, one of us stood up, walked around the mess hall, and wrote "All secure" in the log. At 0400 four other sleepy officers came in and relieved us. We left the mess hall in their care.

It was not that first disillusionment, however, that put Woodley and me "on the tree" the first weekend. A week earlier, before our induction, we would have called it "confinement to the school grounds." Now we used the salty term about the tree. I was being punished for tying poor knots, Woodley for writing poor letters, and Commander Wilson for failing every course he took.

In spite of the difference in rank, we took a protective interest in Wilson. He was a fifty-year-old professor of international law whose book was used on three continents. Having volunteered for the navy's military government program he had been commissioned a commander. Once, in a dejected moment, he remarked that he might have been wiser to accept a colonelcy the army had offered him. He was an urbane, chubby New Englander and he had not been told, when he volunteered, that he would be put through the indoctrination school. Sometimes he was visibly harassed, though we never heard him complain.

One thing that distressed Wilson was the necessity to keep shining his shoes. Our shoes were constantly being inspected. Several times we were dismissed early from class and lined up outdoors so that the officer of the deck, followed by the junior officer of the deck and a yeoman, could inspect our shoes. We all felt that the executive officer had a preposterous affinity for clean shoes, but no one seemed inclined to tell him that. We shined our shoes. All of us, that is, except Wilson. He tried, but he was not overly successful. He had had his shoes shined by servants for so long that he had gotten out of the habit, and he may have felt that at his age he could dispense with it.

But Ensign Bunce disagreed. Having just completed a four-month course at midshipman school, Bunce was assigned to train newly commissioned civilians. He had been an instructor of physical education in a YMCA and he carried the missionary fervor of his former occupation into his new duties.

Bunce accepted no excuses. He regretted that Mr. Wilson had not been able to change from his uniform to his gym-suit in the allotted three minutes, but the penalty for such failure was an hour of drill after dinner. Bunce did not explain how the extra hour of marching would accelerate Wilson's dressing, and at seven o'clock we would sit and watch the commander plodding around, with other miscreants, doing "shoulder arms" and "port arms" and "about face" and the other standard exercises.

Ensign Bunce didn't have to drill the sluggards, for his official day had ended at four o'clock, or, as he insisted, 1600. Bunce stayed over to help win the war. We had been instructed to use naval phraseology at all times and to pretend that the barracks we lived in were ships at sea. We walked decks and ate chow and washed in the head. Within reasonable limits we didn't mind playing this innocuous game but Bunce had no sense of humor. He would shout, to the squad dragging itself wearily across the dusty drill field, "Straighten out the bow. You on the port side, swing starboard. Heads up. Look proud. You're in the navy."

The response from a squad of lawyers, businessmen, and professors was singularly restrained. Most of the student officers at indoctrination school were professional men who had been commissioned directly into the navy. Their ranks ranged from ensign to commander, and off the school grounds those ranks were valid; when Ensign Bunce met Commander Wilson in New York City, Bunce had to salute first. But at the school a different system prevailed, and all student officers wore white hats to distinguish them from the staff. One of the more popular occupations among the students was speculating on getting Bunce as a subordinate officer sometime in the future. He would not have been a happy man undergoing all the tortures to which a naval officer could be subjected.

In a sense, it wasn't Bunce's fault. He and hundreds of hurriedly prepared young ensigns like him had to do the job of training because the navy needed its experienced officers on the ships, doing the fighting. We understood that. And we understood that the fastest way to train thousands of civilians for a complicated job with which they were completely unfamiliar was to drill into them certain basic principles and standard operating procedures. What irritated us was the undiscriminating insistence on following minute regulations, regardless of whether in our particular situation they were relevant, helpful, or sensible. Eager-beaver little officers like Bunce spent many hours lining up hats with buttons, squaring caps, inspecting shoes, and making people run to formations where they then stood and waited. They called musters on every conceivable occasion, and we went through more fire drills and air-raid drills on the edge of New York than most of us went through during the remainder of the war. Because we resented standing frozen at attention while silly little ensigns playing navy meticulously inspected us, we sometimes did silly things ourselves. When an inexperienced platoon leader called out "right face" instead of "left" our whole platoon marched happily into the captain's garden. And to the enraged officer who immediately demanded an explanation, Woodley proudly replied, "Obeying orders, sir."

That first weekend, Wilson, Woodley, and I resolved to be better students. It wasn't easy. In the mechanical-aptitude test Wilson made the lowest grade in the history of the school. His contact with mechanical problems had for a long time been limited to getting caps off bottles and, subsequently, keys into keyholes. Now he discovered that the kind of intelligence he possessed was not only inadequate in solving practical problems, it was usually misleading.

Ensign Tripp, the seamanship instructor, was very patient with Wilson. Trip was a pudgy man with pale blue eyes who wanted badly to go back to sea. He had been asking for sea duty every month. Something, or somebody, was holding up his request. Until it was granted, Tripp had to continue teaching seamanship instead of practicing it. He was a man of considerable self control and he needed all of it when he had to teach Wilson.

"Watch closely, Mr. Wilson," he would say, "I have drawn a ship on the board. The ship is traveling in this direction. Here, where the arrow is pointing. This is a single-screw ship. Now, if this ship runs into a six-knot current, will it turn port or starboard?"

The answer was obvious to Tripp. It seemed obvious to the class. But it wasn't obvious to Wilson. He looked at the ship carefully. There were only two alternatives.

"Port?" he would ask hopefully.

"Starboard," Trip would answer sadly.

Wilson would sit down and Trip would make a little mark in his grade-book and ask someone else another question. Wilson would think hard about the answer to that question and again reach the wrong conclusion.

Sometimes Wilson couldn't, or wouldn't, remember the material in the textbook. He was always affable about his ignorance and said politely, "I don't know, sir." When Trip asked how far a ship would drift under certain conditions, Wilson may have felt that when he flew overseas two months later to serve as an admiral's advisor on international law, he would not be asked how far ships drifted. He may also have foreseen that he would never be in charge of a ship's gunnery division, for when Ensign Bunce asked him at what degree the anti-aircraft guns should be set in a hypothetical situation, Wilson answered courteously, "At the proper one, I presume, sir."

Wilson never did get "off the tree," although for a while it looked as if he might make it the final weekend before graduation. All of his instructors, except Bunce, had agreed to keep his name off the failure list that last time. And since there had been no test in gunnery that week, we looked forward to a farewell spree. But at the final inspection Saturday morning Bunce stopped in front of Wilson, examined him carefully, and said, "Two-block your tie."

"Yes, sir," Wilson said, and yanked at his tie.

Bunce looked at him sternly. "I've been telling you to two-block your tie for seven weeks. You still haven't done it. Sorry. Weekend privileges canceled."

After we had been dismissed I asked Wilson, "Has he really been warning you about your tie?"

"I suppose so," he said unhappily. "Every day he tells me to two-block it."

"Then why didn't you do it?" I asked.

"I don't know what two-block means," he said.

"It just means pull your tie all the way to the top," I told him.

Wilson thought about it for a moment. "I wish people would speak more plainly around here," he said dispiritedly and wandered off to the barracks.

Toward the end of the training period, most of the men had adjusted, temporarily, to the routine. But it was clearly understood that the adjustment was temporary, a kind of armed truce, and the number of days remaining was shouted off loudly every morning.

The indoctrination school offered all of the personal indignities of navy life and none of the psychological compensations of actual service. We had found that in the restricted life at the school little things mattered a great deal. Unexpected irritations caused great unhappiness; unexpected concessions proved extremely gratifying. The arrival of mail became very important, and delay in delivery immediately affected the morale of the corps. The men made life more bearable by living from one high point of expectation to another—a weekend party, a trip, a visit. In civilian life there had been pleasure in simply enjoying the present, but only looking ahead to the future could make the period at the school bearable.

There were exceptions, of course. Ensign Loggers, a bulky, open-mouthed Alabaman, worked hard at everything. Marching was no casual matter for him; he did it stiffly, earnestly, keeping his head up and his chest out and obeying zealously every command that Bunce gave. And Lieutenant Alders didn't seem to be bothered by the routine. Alders was a tanned, wiry Texan, relaxed, good humored, and amoral. It was Alders who, on the day he was platoon leader, changed the cadence-count from "One, two, one, two," to "Lamb stew, lamb stew," an innovation that proved so popular that even Bunce could not eradicate it. And it was Alders who came up with a refreshing reply when he was teased about his armed guard assignment.

"You know the rule for armed guard officers," Woodley said to him. "You have to stay on a sinking ship until the guns are under water."

"Not me," Aldus said emphatically. "I'm leaving a complete set of instructions for the gun crew, but I can't wait that long."

When Wilson was ordered to stay on the base for the final weekend, Woodley and I went to Manhattan without him. This time we got into trouble. There was an inordinate amount of gold braid at the foot of the Battery, for the big Atlantic convoys were assembled there and merchant marine officers converged on the port captain's building. Holland, Norway, England, Sweden, and Free France were among the nations gaudily represented. Since there were no legal restrictions on the amount of gold braid a merchant marine officer could display, everyone who liked that sort of thing wore a gold-leafed cap and sprinkled his sleeves liberally with gold stripes.

Woodley and I were strolling along when we heard a sharp and angry "Attention." We turned and saw a furious little man scowling at us. There were three stars on his cap and two stripes above the solid gold band on his cuff. It was the first time either of us had been addressed by a vice admiral of the United States Navy.

"Don't you salute senior officers?" he asked. The question seemed to mean a good deal to him, and I was about to explain that with so much gold braid on the Battery nobody bothered to salute, when it struck me that that might not be a politic remark to make to an admiral.

"Sorry, sir," Woodley said, "we didn't see you."

The admiral glared at me and I said, "Me too, sir."

"You saw me out of the corner of your eyes," the admiral said.

"No, sir," Woodley said. "Sorry, sir."

"Sorry, sir," I said. "Didn't see you."

"Your name?" the admiral snapped at me.

By this time a fair-sized crowd had surrounded us and was listening to the colloquy with uninhibited delight. I felt, under the circumstances, an irresistible disinclination to reveal personal data.

"Patton, sir," I said. General Patton's army had just won a victory and his name was in the headlines.

"And your name?"

"Patton, sir," Woodley said.

The admiral stared at us. "You're both named Patton?"

"Cousins, sir," Woodley explained.

The admiral hesitated, then said, "Where are you stationed?"

"The P-T boat school," Woodley said.

"Radar school," I said.

"How long have you been in the navy?"

"Since yesterday, sir," Woodley said.

"Last week, sir," I said.

The admiral looked at us for some time. Then he told us what he thought of junior officers who didn't salute admirals. He had strong views on the subject and he revealed them with exceptional clarity to us and to the spectators. Then he dismissed us. We saluted energetically, wheeled rapidly, and marched off. At the first corner we executed a sharp turn, and I've stayed away from the Battery to this day.

During the last week we waited nervously for our next assignment. It was maddening to think that all of our futures were being determined, and some of our deaths made likely, by impersonal decisions of obscure officers in the bureau of personnel who would look at our records and arbitrarily send us to specialized schools, land bases, or armed guard on merchant ships. Some of the men preferred to think that the personnel people were fulfilling a higher destiny than mere bureaucracy. "It doesn't matter where you're sent," Alders said. "If your number is up, you'll get it. If it isn't, you'll be safer on armed guard duty than on a land base."

I noticed that Woodley was one of the few men who didn't show the slightest concern. When his orders to report to advanced small boat school came, he seemed very pleased. I was ordered to communications school and spent a lot of time rationalizing, with most of the other men, about the next assignment. We managed to convince ourselves that we were no worse off than other people.

Things suddenly eased up at the school. For seven weeks we had not been permitted to sit on our beds between 6 A.M. and 10 P.M., even after we had been given typhoid injections. But now that we were strong, healthy, and had nothing to do, we could lie down any time.

For the graduation ceremony we were ordered to buy white gloves. I don't know whether any of my classmates ever used them again, but I didn't and Woodley didn't. Some men grumbled about this outdated requirement, but we both felt that the two farewell addresses compensated for it. The first was a speech by the president of the borough where the school was located. He used every platitude about patriotism and unselfish service and the heroism of battle that anyone had ever used; he made the V-for-victory sign with his fingers; and he finally got so carried away that he forgot he was not addressing a civilian audience and implored us to think of the boys in service and stop complaining to his office about rationing.

The captain's speech was brief. During the following three years I was to hear many variations of this military principle, but never as succinctly as in its original Annapolis form. "Gentlemen," the captain said, "keep your mouth shut; your eyes, ears, and bowels open; and don't volunteer for a goddamn thing."

Chapter 3

Five months later Woodley and I were on a train to Seattle. He had finished the course in small boats and I had completed my training in communications school. We had just ordered drinks in the crowded club car when a navy aviator and a girl asked if they could share our booth. The flier, a burly man with a square, bronzed face, told us that his name was Merkle. The girl, whom he had just met, was Eva Jensen. She had the regular, vacuous features of a porcelain doll and short blond hair. She wore a lot of lipstick and a tight sweater. She was about twenty-two and told us that she was on her way to join a USO dance troupe in Seattle.

Merkle asked where we were going.

"You know how the navy works," Woodley said. "I graduated from crash-boat school and asked for duty in the South Pacific. Last week I got my orders.

"Well?"

"Aleutians," Woodley said.

"How about you?" Merkle said.

"I asked for the European theater," I said.

"Yeh? Where're you going?"

"Aleutians."

"Well," Eva said, "if my troupe ever gets out there I'll look you boys up."

"I'll count on that," Woodley said. His hand groped for hers under the table but didn't reach it. Merkle was holding it.

"From what I hear about the Aleutians, you'll be glad to see a woman after you've been there a while," she said.

"I'll be glad to see you," Woodley said.

"Rugged up there," Merkle said. "No women. Friend of mine came back after a year, shacked up with a broad, didn't come out for two weeks."

Eva said, musingly, "A girl could make a lot more than seventy-five USO bucks a week up there."

"That's a fact," said Merkle. He had released her hand and was rubbing her knee. "You sure could."

"Where are you going?" Woodley asked Merkle.

"Seattle. A couple of days there, then back to the air station in Miami."

"Secret mission?"

"Nothing secret. Roommate crashed. Training flight. I'm taking the body to the family. Navy sent me."

Eva caught the steward's eye and ordered a refill. "You mean the coffin is on this train?" she asked.

"Baggage car," Merkle said. "Family meets me at the station. I turn it over and stay for the funeral, makes them feel better."

"What kind of guy was he?" Woodley asked.

"Who?"

"Your roommate. The guy who got killed."

"OK," Merkle said. He was holding Eva's hand again and rubbing his finger in a circular motion against her palm.

"How old?" Woodley asked.

"About twenty. Nice kid but had a lot to learn. Know what I mean?" Woodley said. "Enthused about everything. Crazy about flying. Called it adventure."

"Don't you like flying?"

Merkle seemed surprised. "No," he said. "Nothing special. I fly good so I do it. It pays pretty good."

"And you're taking his coffin back to his folks," Eva said. She snuggled closer to Merkle.

"That's right."

"I'm sorry about your roommate," Woodley said. "It's—I don't know, it's pathetic getting killed in a training flight. You feel it's wasted."

"Yeh?" Merkle said.

"I mean, if he had to die, he'd rather die in battle. I know I would."

"You would?"

"Of course I would," Woodley said. "I don't know about your roommate, but I'm sure that there's a purpose in my life."

"There is?"

Woodley spoke slowly, "I know that this is hard to believe, but I've been saved by miracles twice. When I was a little boy my school burned down. There were twelve children in the room and the teacher. She died and six of the kids died. I wasn't hurt at all."

"What do you know," said Merkle.

"Shut up," Eva said. "I want to hear this. What was the other time?"

"We went on a canoe trip one summer. The boat tipped over. The boy with me drowned."

"What did you do?" Merkle asked.

"I held on to the canoe till help came."

"What's the miracle?" Merkle said. "You were tougher, that's all."

Woodley shook his head. "No. There was a reason. I think God is saving me for some special purpose."

No one said anything. Then Eva stood up. "If you gentlemen will excuse me, I have to go powder my nose."

Merkle ordered another drink.

"She's a nice kid," Woodley said.

"She'll lay," Merkle said.

"I don't think so," Woodley said. "She's different."

Merkle smiled. "All broads are the same."

I asked him what he had done before the war. "Investigator for the Treasury," he said. "You know, G-man stuff."

"Interesting work?"

"It paid pretty good. Funny case we had with a girl in Kansas City. This Eva reminds me of her."

"Tell us," Woodley said.

"We're looking for a guy for forgery. We got his wallet, with a picture of a babe holding her skirt up above her belly, nothing on underneath. Her address is on the back of the picture. We're waiting in her room when she comes home from work. She's a beauty operator.

"'Where's Henry Lawson?' I ask her.

"'Who the hell is he?' she says.

"I showed her Lawson's picture.

"'Oh him,' she says. 'I remember the guy. I had a date with him once.'

"'Don't give me that crap,' I say. 'If you only met him once, how come he's got an intimate photo of you?'

"'Intimate photo?' she says. Then she grins. 'Oh, you mean like this?' And she lifts her skirt above her belly."

Merkle laughed. Woodley said, "I don't see why Eva reminds you of that girl. Does she look like her?"

"She don't look like her," Merkle said.

Eva came back and Merkle put his arm around her waist. "Do you have to unload that coffin?" she asked.

"Family'll be there," Merkle said. "They'll take care of it."

"Is this the first time you escorted a body?" Woodley asked.

"First time, last time, what's the difference? Orders is orders."

"You hear stories about silly orders," Woodley said. "A guy named Nolan graduated from indoctrination school with us. His orders said, 'Proceed immediately' to Great Lakes. The rest of us got five days' leave and two days' travel time. But not Nolan. He had a cab waiting at the graduation hall. The minute the ceremony was finished he raced across town to the airport, caught a plane for Chicago, took the train to

Great Lakes, and reported that afternoon. He's still there. I saw him the other day and he told me about it."

"Why did they want him in such a hurry?" Eva asked.

"I don't know," Woodley said, "Nobody knows. He rushed into the O.O.D.'s office end reported. The O.O.D. signed him in and told him to come back the next day. Nolan insisted that somebody must have wanted him badly to make him fly across the country like that. So the O.O.D. found the personnel officer and the personnel officer told Nolan to relax and come back the next day."

"What's he doing there?" Eva asked.

"He's in a room full of officers. They're all waiting for assignments. While they wait they grade correspondence courses. Nolan is grading international law."

"Nolan doesn't know anything about international law," I said.

"He doesn't have to. All he has to do is check the answer sheets with a scoring key. The exam is based on a book written in 1927, so everybody who answers on the basis of actual conditions has to be marked wrong. For instance, the textbook says bombing of civilians is prohibited."

"That's a hot one," Merkle said.

"But Nolan says most of the officers who take the course get perfect scores."

"Right," Merkle said. "Copy the answers from a guy who's taken the course. Only way to do it."

"I still don't know why they wanted that Nolan in such a hurry," Eva said.

"You'll never know," Merkle told her. "Nobody'll ever know. Don't worry about it."

"I don't get it," she said. "Is that all these guys do, grade papers?"

"Not all of them," Woodley said. "The ones who don't grade papers are correcting navy regs. That's the bible. If you do anything that's not in navy regs you're out of luck. It's made up of hundreds of loose-leaf pages put together in 1920. The big job now is keeping it up to date, because Washington sends out corrections, revisions, and cancellations every day."

"No use," Merkel said. "They'll never catch up."

"Well, they're not trying too hard. Nolan says the guy in charge of the office is regular navy, a commander retired for disability. He feels that this operation is so far from real navy that he doesn't even want to pretend it's a military establishment. So they all take it easy, read the papers in the morning, have coffee at 9, milk and cookies at 10, knock off for lunch at 11. In the afternoon they watch baseball games or go swimming. Nolan's so bored he's read all the comic books on the base."

"Well, boys," Eva said, "if you're gonna talk about books I better move along."

"Where?" Woodley asked.

"I got a roomette."

Merkle stood up and took her arm. "Let's go."

"Not right now," she said, smiling up at him. Then she turned to us. "I'll see you boys at dinner."

After she left, Merkle took out a deck of cards. We played for a while.

"You in communications, Jack?" Merkle said.

I nodded. "Heard a funny one about you guys," he said. "Always harping on security. Never leave the codes out. Never let unauthorized personnel see the stuff. Very important. Right?"

"That's right."

"Well, you boys helped organize a convoy out of New York. A lot of foreign ships. One Latvian skipper, didn't know much English. The communications officer told him to keep all the comm publications in the safe. Guard it with his life. Skipper says fine, he understands. He'll take personal charge of those pubs. Nobody is going to see them, not even the radio operator. Hell no, says the comm officer, you gotta let the radio operator see them or he can't break messages. OK, says the skipper, he'll let the radio operator use them. And don't let those pubs fall overboard, the comm officer tells him. Mustn't lose them in the water. The skipper says OK.

"The convoy's attacked and the ships scatter. A German sub catches up with the Latvian ship. The men shove off in lifeboats. Sub sinks ship, sends for the skipper. The sub commander wants to ask him some questions. Skipper goes aboard the sub, carrying a steel box. The Germans ask what he's got in it. They're secret pubs, he tells them. That comm officer told him not to lose them and by God he didn't."

Merkle stood up. "That the way you guys do business? Lots of foul-ups. Well, I got to clean up. See you later."

Woodley and I went back to the Pullman and watched the flat countryside, snow fences, and windbreaks. Then Woodley said, "It's five o'clock. Let's get Eva and eat."

"Give her a little time," I said. "It's too early to eat."

"No. She should be ready."

We washed up and then Woodley knocked on the door of Eva's roomette. No one answered. He knocked again. After a long moment Eva called out, "Who is it?"

Woodley told her, We heard a thud in the room, as if someone heavy had stood up, then the sound of whispering. Finally Eva called out, "Wait for me in the lounge, I'll be there in a few minutes."

We sat in the lounge. After a while Merkle joined us. "We're waiting for Eva," Woodley told him.

"I'll wait with you," Merkle said gravely.

Eva seemed tired when she finally appeared. She had changed clothes. In the dinner line she turned to Merkle. "If there's a train wreck or something, are you responsible for the coffin?"

"I guess so," Merkle said. "How do you feel now?"

She looked at him and giggled, then turned to Woodley. "Do your crash boats go awful fast?"

He said, so softly that I could hardly hear him, "Can I see you tonight?"

She smiled pleasantly. "Not tonight, honey."

He frowned, and she squeezed his hand. "I couldn't make it, honey. Maybe tomorrow night."

The following evening I fell asleep before Woodley came to bed, and the train arrived in Seattle early in the morning. While we packed hurriedly, Woodley said, "She's a swell girl, Jack. She's going to try to get to the Aleutians with her USO troupe. In the meantime she promised to write."

That afternoon we took a navy plane to Adak.

Chapter 4

Woodley was the officer in charge of crash boats, and he had a desk in our office in the port captain's building. Whenever a plane went down, or a ship got into trouble, or a quick investigation of offshore waters was required, the crash boats were ordered out. Woodley loved these sudden orders. He would run out of the office, jump down to the crash boat dock, and give commands. A moment later his boat would race noisily out of the harbor, leaving a churning wake behind it.

But most of his time Woodley had to spend at his desk, doing "administrative" work. And since he disliked paper work now even more than he had at indoctrination school, he wasn't really happy in the office. What irritated him most was the squawk box.

The squawk box was a small machine on Commander Pierce's desk that was connected for oral communication with seven other offices on the base. The pushbuttons identifying these offices were arranged in the order of diminishing importance. The captain's office was number one. It was easy to recognize which office Commander Pierce was addressing by the tone of his voice. If it was polite and self-deprecating, he was talking to one or two, the latter being the executive officer. When Pierce addressed the captain's aide, he was affectionately genial. Pompous seriousness marked his conversation with the personnel officer, and his remarks to the harbormaster were curt. The security officer was spoken to sharply, as a subordinate who sometimes forgot to keep his place. And when the commander talked to number seven, the ship's clerk, it was with aloof and contemptuous efficiency.

The commander's attitude toward each pushbutton on the squawk box did not change, regardless of who actually replied. The commander spoke to the enlisted man in the captain's office with the same respect he gave the captain. And his language to number seven was always scathing, until on one unfortunate occasion he pressed the wrong button and was informed, by a sputtering squawk box, "I am not in the habit, commander, of being called a dumb bastard by my subordinate officers."

According to proper procedure, the originator of the conversation was supposed to identify himself at the start. The captain, however, frequently ignored proper procedure and barked commands into the box without any preliminaries. Once, he was not heard because someone else was talking on another circuit. The captain burst into our office a few minutes later and angrily asked why he hadn't been answered. Our explanation was logical but not acceptable. After that we always kept an ear open for the captain's voice.

In the morning, Woodley and I rode down to the port captain's building with Commander Pierce. Only the captain and the executive officer had reserved parking spots. Pierce would park the jeep in the spot next to the executive officer's. He insisted on getting his jeep into that spot if it was at all possible to squeeze the jeep in. On days when someone else had parked there he grumbled about usurpers who lacked proper respect for rank, and he was short-tempered the rest of the morning. The spot where the commander managed to park made a good deal of difference in the atmosphere at the office.

When we stepped into the office at eight o'clock, Manley, the yeoman; Warren and Nooters, the quartermasters; and Mason, the messenger, were there, busily at work. Lieutenant Dutton, Pierce's assistant, was at his desk; and Ensign Edwards, the minesweeping officer, and Lieutenant (junior grade) King, the boarding officer, were usually at theirs. The commander had once reprimanded Edwards for tardiness, before he learned that Edwards' father owned a large department store in Chicago.

The men usually thought of each other as single, unattached individuals, but we were always aware of Dutton's family. There was a large picture of his wife and son on his office desk. He had a good-sized photo of them in his room. And when he took out his wallet we could see the cellophaned snapshot of the woman and the boy. Dutton was a thin, stooped-shouldered, aloof man with a thin blond mustache.

The enlisted men hated him.

I remember Nooters standing sullenly by Dutton's desk while Dutton told him what he thought of him. In his eagerness to be helpful, Nooters sometimes embarked on dusting expeditions. The office was clean but Nooters got tired of sitting around and energetically dusted everything in the room. In the process he often mislaid papers and upset our filing system.

We usually ignored the damage. But not Dutton. He told Nooters that he was a useless moron. The charge had a large element of truth in it, although it might have been expressed more tactfully. Later, when Dutton had gone, Nooters mumbled, "If I ever find that son-of-a-bitch after the war I'll kill him."

"Don't do that," Warren said, "Just cut his balls off."

Nooters was not open to dissuasion. "No," he insisted, "I'll kill him."

Commander Pierce had been a theater manager in civilian life. He looked older than he was, and there was always a trace of artificial politeness in his manner to strangers. He kept worrying that something, somewhere, might not have been done correctly, and he kept double-checking. As a result of that constant fidgeting of his, everything at the office was done with much more fretting than was necessary.

The commander read the night's dispatches and passed them on to me. I took whatever action I was, as routing officer, supposed to. Then I read the newspapers that had been flown up from Seattle. At nine-thirty the commander usually stepped over to the administration building. Mason made coffee and listened to the latest scuttlebutt. The men talked slowly, lazily, refilling their coffee cups leisurely. If there was a profound difference between veterans and civilians, as some experts after the war claimed, it was not apparent in our office. The men talked about sex and major league baseball and the probable length of the war. Their views on all three subjects were not strikingly original.

Lately Manley had said very little. He was a small man in his thirties who had been a clerk in civilian life. He was still a clerk, though the navy called clerks yeomen. Manley was very worried about his wife. Now that he had been overseas a year, her letters arrived less and less frequently. His mother had recently written, hinting that Mrs. Manley was seeing another man. Manley had immediately tried to get an emergency leave, but the commander told him to wait a while and see what happened. Manley's eyes gleamed through the ugly brass-rimmed G-I glasses and he tapped his foot nervously while he listened to the men talk, a stooped, sad, timid little man. He was an excellent yeoman and could have done most of the work in the office by himself.

Twenty-year-old Warren was always in good spirits. He was a quarter-master second class, a bright young man who was planning to go to college after the war and would probably have done a good deal of accurate quarter-mastering for us if we had needed it. We needed very little, so Warren spent much of his time at the office writing letters to movie actresses, asking for photographs, and to girls he knew, asking for dates in the distant future. He played baseball in summer, football in fall, and basketball in winter. When there was no athletic competition scheduled, or a USO show, he went to movies. He saw an astonishing number of movies.

Even Commander Pierce approved of the correspondence with Hollywood, for it kept Warren busy. Warren arrived at the office at 0730. He dusted, opened the windows, and arranged the dispatches and newspapers neatly on the commander's desk. Then he looked around earnestly for something to do. Sometimes he asked Manley whether there was anything he could do. By this time Manley had opened his typewriter, put in a clean sheet of paper, and begun typing a letter home. Manley could never suggest anything that had to be done. Warren would take out his list of movie stars and begin composing a letter to one of them.

It was a point of honor with Warren to write an original letter to each of his beautiful correspondents. Some of the men on the base used form letters, made twenty copies, and sent them to Hollywood. Not Warren. He worked slowly on each letter, pausing sometimes to bite the pencil and stare wistfully off into space. Once, when he was finding creation difficult, I suggested a word he might use. He looked at me suspiciously, said "Thank you, sir," and ignored my suggestion. Later Ensign Edwards told me that Warren had once asked him for help in writing to his girl. Edwards had offered the phrase "My defecating darling" as an original method of addressing a sweetheart. Warren wrote it down gratefully and mailed the letter. After that, I noticed, Warren frequently used the dictionary.

Warren's longest letters were written to a girl named Edith in San Francisco. To Edith's sister, who was twelve years older, married, and apparently interested in the youngsters' romance, he wrote briefer notes. Warren wanted to go steady with Edith but couldn't get her to agree. She felt that at nineteen she was too young to be tied down. Warren regretted this flightiness and sometimes speculated aloud about Edith's virginity. The older boys gave him advice, and the officers volunteered to explain the facts of life to him. Warren nodded gratefully and politely asked for more information. We gave it, smugly, until one day the San Francisco papers carried a story about Edith's sister. She was being sued for divorce, and the correspondent listed was a quartermaster named Warren. Edith's sister admitted in court that Warren had proved so much more adept sexually than her husband that she no longer had any interest in said husband.

Mason, the messenger, was a squat, slow-moving, graying man who had requested a second tour of duty on Adak when his eighteen months were up. He was a petty-officer first class; his wife and four children received an allotment; and he boasted of making more money in the service than he ever had in civilian life. He was very prompt with his "yes, sirs"; he carried out orders efficiently; he was polite and helpful; and I didn't trust him.

Nooters, quartermaster third class, was the other enlisted man in the office.

My main job as routing officer was to provide sailing orders to every merchant vessel that sailed in Aleutian waters. But since there wasn't too much shipping during the last year of the war, I had been assigned a few additional tasks, such as the compiling of monthly reports. Most of the reports were repetitious, and all that was necessary was to change the name of the month. But the small-boat report did vary. Sometimes a boat was sunk, or damaged, or surveyed. I had to record that fact on my list each month.

Manley, the yeoman, could have done the job as well as I. Warren, the quartermaster, could have done it. In an emergency, anyone in the office except Nooters could have done it. But we had a lot of time and reports were official business, so officers were delegated to do them. One month, to test my suspicion that no one read these reports, I put into the middle pages of the landing-craft summary a few sentences about Joe DiMaggio's batting average, Kant's categorical imperative, and the regulation of concubines in China. When I brought the report into the captain's office he initialed it and told his yeoman to send it on through the chain of command. I don't know who was supposed to read it next, but I never heard a word about it.

I did hear about another report I had submitted. The first intimation came over the squawk box. It was a sharp "Pierce, come in here." The commander said "Yes, sir" and ran down to the captain's office. He looked a little pale when he left and he was red-faced when he came back.

He threw a batch of papers on my desk and snapped, "How do you account for this, Mr. Ward?"

"What is it?" I asked.

"It's your boat report. Why isn't the admiral's boat listed on it?"

I checked through the list quickly. There was no sign of the admiral's boat, yet I was sure that I had listed it.

"I'll check on it," I said.

Pierce looked at his wristwatch. "You have one hour, lieutenant. I expect this error explained by that time."

"Yes, sir," I said, and shuffled through the papers again. The commander glowered. His face was still very red.

"The admiral himself found that mistake," he said. "He checked the report this morning and noticed that his own boat was not listed. He really got angry."

"Did he talk to the captain about it?" I asked.

The commander was still scowling. "No. He gave his chief of staff the word."

I kept looking through the report. The commander picked up his pencil a couple of times and put it down. Then he looked at me again. "The chief of staff called the captain and bawled him out. Now the captain's mad."

"Yes, sir," I said.

"The captain was pretty nasty. He said if certain people don't get the lead out of their ass he is going to make some changes around here."

I looked through the report again, this time going from back to front. "I'm warning you, lieutenant," Pierce said. "Get the lead out and explain this or there are going to be some changes around here."

I turned to the yeoman. "Manley," I said, "Did you type this report?"

Manley looked at it. "I guess I did. It has my initials on it."

"Ah," I said.

"It has your initials too," he said.

"Oh. Well, where is the original you copied this from?"

Manley began to look for the original in his files. He couldn't find it and turned to Warren. "Where did you put that report?" he asked.

Warren was started. "I don't know anything about it. I don't touch your files."

"Yeh," Manley said. "You better get the lead out around here."

The commander glared at me; I glared at Manley; Manley glared at Warren; and Warren looked miserable. Then I looked at the first page of the report again and smiled.

"Commander," I said, "I think I have the answer."

"Proceed, lieutenant," he said.

"This is the report for December. It's July now. I didn't list the admiral's boat in December because we didn't have it then. It arrived from the States in April."

Pierce came over to my desk. "Is that right, Ward?"

"That's right."

He took the report and ran down to the captain's office. When he came back a half hour later he was smiling benignly.

"Well, Jack," he said, "That certainly was a funny one. Yes, sir, that was a good one, spotting that date."

"What got the admiral so excited?" I asked.

"Why, he had nothing to do when he came into his office this morning, so he just reached into a stack of reports lying in a file and came up with this one. He hadn't seen any reports before this one and he hasn't seen any since. I guess he was trying to show us he was keeping close watch on things."

The commander went off for his morning coffee and a few minutes later, promptly at ten as always, Major Drewry strode into the room and said, "Good morning, lieutenant. May I have the ship-movement report for today?"

Major Drewry was attached to the army's coast artillery unit, which conducted practice shooting on days when visibility permitted it. This unit was supposed to use our daily report as a guide to avoid hitting our ships. Inasmuch as the artillery fired only on clear days, when they themselves could see the ships, and since our reports were never accurate within four hours, the usefulness of the report was questionable. But the artillery unit had always been given a report; it sent the major over every day; and we gave him the report.

I said, "Good morning, major. Here is your report. Have a cup of coffee?"

"Sorry," he snapped. "I'm in a hurry. My driver is waiting in the jeep. I have to get back to maneuvers."

"Have a cup of coffee," I repeated.

The major hesitated. "Oh, all right. I'll have just one cup." He took off his cap, put the report in it, and sat down. While Mason poured the coffee the major pulled out a cigarette case, offered

Woodley and me a smoke, tapped the case, said casually, "Gold, you know. My father-in-law gave it to me," and leaned back comfortably.

Sometimes, if he was still sitting there at noon, I invited him to eat with us. He always accepted. Army food was not very good, he explained apologetically. Sometimes he left by 1130, announcing that he had to get back to maneuvers. The driver had been waiting outside in the jeep.

Occasionally Woodley and I wandered down the hall to the O.O.D. room to visit Lieutenant Krueger. Krueger was the permanent officer of the deck; his job consisted chiefly of sitting in the O.O.D. office all day. He had to be there at 0800 to watch the marines raise the flag, and he had to be there at 1800 to watch them lower it. And he had to be there at noon to test the siren. If ever the Japanese invaded the island, the siren would give the general alarm. Its daily testing was a rigid requirement on the base. At first I had been startled by the sudden high-pitched screech that wailed across the island, set the dogs howling, and woke the men resting after night watches. After a while I was scarcely conscious of it, except on Sundays. When we had a change of command the new captain, who stayed up late Saturday nights, eliminated the Sunday siren.

Krueger spent most of his time as O.O.D. reading newspapers, magazines, and comics. I once asked him why he didn't read books, and he said that he had tried once, early in his O.O.D. career, but the captain had seen him and told him it was undignified for an officer to read books on duty.

Once, while we were visiting him, Krueger asked us to take care of things while he slipped out of the office. I sat down in the swivel chair. Four telephones, a large log, and Woodley rested on the desk. The telephones were distinguished by the tones of their ringing, but I wasn't familiar enough with them to be able to distinguish among them. When one of the phones rang, I picked up the nearest one and said "Hello," but no one answered. I was about to put it down and try another when I saw Woodley signaling me to be careful. The captain was standing in the door watching me. He looked angry and it occurred to me that this was no time to be fumbling for phones. I embarked on a businesslike but entirely one-sided conversation with my telephone. One of the other phones kept ringing. The captain finally went away. After that I tried not to be alone in the O.O.D's office, even when I learned to recognize which phone was ringing.

Krueger wanted to be informed whenever ships sailed from Adak to San Francisco. I would tell him that the *Cavanaugh* was scheduled to go to San Francisco the following morning. He would ask all about the ship: what it looked like; who was the captain; what speed it made. Then he would calculate aloud. "Let's see. At fourteen knots it should be in San Francisco by next Saturday. Probably early Saturday morning, coming in under that bridge through the Golden Gate. Man."

The next time there was a sailing to San Francisco I would inform him, and again he would ask about the ship and plot it all the way. I once remarked to the commander that Krueger must be very lonesome for his hometown to be so curious about it. The commander laughed. "Lonesome, hell. Krueger has never seen San Francisco. He comes from Cedar Rapids, Iowa."

I hadn't come from Iowa, but my civilian training hadn't given me any more knowledge about my navy job than Krueger had about San Francisco. Much of my work consisted of dealing with the merchant marine. I gave the captains routing instructions, and the officers of merchant ships came in to take the communications test. The peace-time procedure of signaling had been superseded by a new system, and all the merchant marine officers had to pass the new test by a given date or face the threat of not having their licenses renewed.

There was some irony in the situation. Having learned the new communications system in a month, and never having sailed aboard a merchant ship, I was examining men who had spent up to forty years at sea. The masters took the test with varying degrees of grace.

One genial, middle-aged captain came bustling in, accompanied by King. King said, "Lieutenant Ward, I want you to meet Captain Green, an old friend of mine. He is skipper of the *Moravia*."

Green pumped my hand, pulled up a chair, and sat down. "Well, well, lieutenant," he beamed. "Certainly glad to meet you. King's been telling me a lot of fine things about you. You'll have to come to dinner on the ship tonight. Yes, sir."

I thanked the captain.

"Not at all," he boomed. "Going to have porterhouse tonight. Don't suppose you've been seeing that kind of meat. Glad to have you. And some Scotch. Don't suppose you object to Scotch, do you, lieutenant?"

I said I didn't object.

"Now about this test the navy wants us to take. King here tells me it's just a technicality. Eh?"

I explained it was more than that. All merchant-marine officers had to learn the new system of communications.

The captain smiled. "Oh well, that's all right. I've got a comm officer on my ship who is up on all that stuff. But I suppose you want me to go through the motions anyway. That's all right." He winked. "Bring it on, lieutenant."

When I had graded his paper and informed him, politely, that he hadn't quite passed, he turned red, grabbed his cap, and stomped out. King asked sadly, "Couldn't you fix it up for him?"

"He hasn't answered one tenth of the questions," I told him. "What could I do?"

King walked out dejectedly. I didn't eat dinner on board ship that night.

Another time the master of a small coastal vessel and his second mate came in to take the test. Captain Hansen was a tall, gaunt Norwegian who had been master of the same little ship for fifteen years. The mate was a young man from Massachusetts who finished his test quickly and passed it easily. I made out his certificate and congratulated him. Then we waited for Captain Hansen to finish.

We waited a long time. The captain was wearing a pair of steel-rimmed spectacles and squinting suspiciously at every letter. He read slowly; he thought slowly; and he wrote slowly. Then he reread each question and thought about it again. Everyone in the office had gone for the day except King, the second mate, and me. We sat there, smoking, trying not to disturb the captain.

As he worked I wondered what I should do. The test was concerned largely with communications procedures in a convoy. The captain's little ship had never been in a convoy and it was not likely that it ever would be, unless the slowest convoy of the war was formed. He had been studying for the test diligently for six months, the mate told me.

Finally he finished. I graded his paper, congratulated him, and made out the certificate. The captain put away his glasses, shook hands with King, the mate, and me and invited us aboard his ship for supper. We had a pleasant meal and the captain brought out a bottle of good brandy. We drank for a while and then I said, "Captain, I've been meaning to ask you. Is the route I've been giving you in your routing orders satisfactory?"

Captain Hansen looked at his mate and they both grinned. "I don't know," the captain said.

"Why not?" I asked.

"I never take it," he said. "I've been sailing Alaskan waters for thirty-four years. If it makes the navy guys in Washington feel better to give me a route, that's OK with me. I don't want to hurt nobody's feelings." He paused to fill his glass, drank it slowly and happily, and patted me on the back. "You're a nice fellow," he said.

"You just keep right on giving me routing instructions. I got nothing against them."

When we rode back home that night King asked, "Did Hansen really pass or did you give him a break?"

"He came close enough," I told him. I felt there wasn't much the navy could teach Captain Hansen.

Nor was there much I ever managed to teach the soldiers on the island of Ogliuga. Every port in Alaska sent us notice of ship movements, except Ogliuga. When a ship departed from Dutch Harbor, Dutch Harbor notified us by dispatch. When a ship arrived at Kodiak, Kodiak sent us word. Even Seguim, a very small base, regularly reported ship movements. The dispatches from Seguim usually arrived a day or two after the ship itself, but the intention was good and you knew where you stood with Seguim.

But not with Ogliuga. We could never be sure what was going on in Ogliuga. An army outpost on that tiny island was supposed to be keeping an eye out for Japs, or gathering weather data, or something, but we never received a dispatch from Ogliuga. At the beginning of each month the captain of the small army freighter *Begonia* came to the port office and asked me for routing orders to Ogliuga. He was a sergeant in the transportation corps and, strictly speaking, should not have been called a captain. But

I had learned early in my naval career that the commanding officer of any vessel could be addressed as captain. It seemed an amiable custom to me and I called everybody captain. Nobody whom I called captain ever corrected me.

Sergeant Kilden had been making the monthly round trip to Ogliuga before I had arrived in the Aleutians. Nobody else ever went to Ogliuga. I had never been within a hundred miles of it. But the regulations required that every vessel leaving Adak had to get routing orders from the port office, so Sergeant Kilden came in and asked for his orders.

"I can have them ready in an hour, captain," I said. "Do you want to wait?"

"No, sir," the sergeant said. "I have a lot of work to do. I'll come back in an hour."

"Right," I said, and he saluted and went away and came back in an hour.

There were times when I had qualms of conscience about this procedure. The orders for Ogliuga were always lying in the bottom drawer of my desk. I could have taken them out, inserted the date in the blank space, put the weather forecast in the envelope, and given the sergeant his orders immediately. If I weren't there, even the yeoman could have done it. The commander, however, was convinced that we would lose a great deal of dignity if the whole business were made as casual as that.

I don't know how helpful my instructions to the sergeant were. My predecessor had established the routing orders to Ogliuga and I never changed them. For voyages by small vessels to unimportant ports, instead of specifying points in longitude and latitude, the orders would read, "Proceed close along the north side of the Aleutian chain to Kanga," or "Proceed south of the chain to Amchitka." With Ogliuga we took no chances and the sergeant's orders always read, "Proceed either north or south of the chain to Ogliuga."

I used to begin the orders with the phrase, "On 10 June, proceed . . ." etc. On one occasion something on the *Begonia* broke down and was not repaired until after midnight. Sergeant Kildon traced me to my hut, woke me up, and asked whether he had to get a new set of orders, reading "On 11 June . . ." etc. After that his orders began with the phrase, "On or about ____, proceed . . ." etc.

When the little ship, Sargeant Kildon commanding, departed from the outer harbor, I would write up a departure dispatch and send it to the communications office. Once, early in my Aleutian career, I sent that dispatch as soon as the ship cleared the inner harbor. That was a mistake. A few minutes later the *Begonia* stopped, turned around, and came back. Later, Sergeant Kildon told me that he had forgotten to load some of the food for Ogliuga. Since the primary purpose of the *Begonia's* voyage was to bring food to Ogliuga, this explanation surprised me. But the sergeant never seemed surprised by anything. He was solemn and stolid and respectful, and he said that his ship had come back to load food.

I don't really know why the *Begonia* came back, nor did I know that the ship had come back until the following morning, when I looked at the army dock and saw a small freighter that looked very much like the *Begonia*. I said to Nooters, "Doesn't that look like the *Begonia?*"

"Sir?" said Nooters."

I repeated my question.

Nooters looked in the direction of the dock. "Yes, sir," he said. "It sure does look like the *Begonia.*"

I didn't know then that all ships looked alike to Nooters. He was near-sighted and excitable. The moment an officer spoke to him, Nooters began to nod enthusiastically, regardless of what was being said.

"Why wasn't I told she came back?" I asked.

"You sure should have been told, sir," Nooters said.

I sent another dispatch, telling Ogliuga that the *Begonia* had not departed. And later in the day, I wrote a third dispatch, informing Ogliuga that the ship had finally gone. Now that I look back on it, I'm not sure it was all worth doing. The men at the communications office went to a good deal of trouble over these dispatches of mine. They checked them for correctness of naval diction; they typed them up; they coded them; they sent them on the air in the form of dots and dashes; they made numerous carbon copies. The admiral looked at them; his chief of staff looked at them; our captain looked at them. Presumably the Japanese intelligence people were listening in, copying the code, and trying to break it down.

There is something fascinating in the notion of enthusiastic Japanese breaking down the dispatches, crypt-analyzing them, and translating them. They could hardly have taken those three messages about the *Begonia* at their face value. They must have thought that something far more important than the voyage of the little freighter was involved. I wonder sometimes what effect my series of dispatches on the *Begonia* had on the eventual outcome of the war.

The dispatches reached our navy, and may have reached the Japanese navy, but they apparently never reached Ogliuga. The war went on, admirals scolded, generals complained. Ogliuga ignored everything with an impenetrable indifference. After I had grown accustomed to Ogliuga's refusal to report ship movements, I anticipated it. But I learned the hard way.

The first time I sent the *Begonia* to Ogliuga I kept track of her on the ship-plot in the port office. The voyage should have taken eighteen hours. Three days later, having received no arrival notice, I checked with the army officials. "It's OK," a major told me. "Don't worry about it. She got there." So I took the disc that represented the *Begonia* off the board and forgot about her.

A week later I was called to the telephone late in the evening. Commander Pierce wanted to know what vessels were approaching Adak. I told him.

"We have accounted for all those ships," he said, "but there is still an unidentified vessel skirting the island." It was too dark to send up a plane to check on the strange ship. Radar had picked it up.

I went down to the port office. The captain was there, the executive officer, and Pierce. We kept in touch with the radar operator and traced the ship to a point north of the island, close to shore. Then it stopped.

The captain said to the executive officer, "What do you think of it?"

"I don't like it," he said. "They may be landing spies."

"Better notify the admiral," said the captain, and went back to his office.

The executive officer turned to Pierce. "Notify the admiral," he said.

"I'm not getting mixed up with the admiral," Pierce said. "Ward, call his aide."

It took me some time to find the aide, at the army club on the other side of the island. He usually spent his evenings at the navy club, but that night he was drinking with the army. "The admiral is pissed off about something," he told me. "I don't want to bother him. Why don't you get a search party organized? Then I can tell him you're taking steps."

I told Pierce what the aide said; Pierce told the executive officer; the executive officer informed the captain; and the captain said, "I knew you couldn't count on that S.O.B." He glared at Pierce. "What the hell are you doing about it?"

"I've sent the patrol craft to investigate. They'll let me know as soon as they contact the vessel."

The captain was still upset. By this time of evening he would ordinarily have had a couple of drinks. "That's not enough," he said. "Get a search party on land organized. Call the general. Hell, this is his god-damned island."

Technically this was true. The army had charge of land operations on Adak. The general was informed. He immediately ordered the antiaircraft units to their stations, sent out scouting parties, and alerted the entire army force. Phones began ringing; jeeps raced; a plane took off, flew around for a while, and then the pilot sent word that he couldn't see anything.

Pierce bustled around the office. "Send out all the PC's," he told me. I ordered all the patrol craft on ready duty to proceed north of the island. At that moment Woodley stepped into the office, by chance, and Pierce saw him.

"What the hell are you doing here?" he yelled. "Get your crash boat out there and investigate."

Woodley didn't know what he was supposed to investigate but he obviously felt that this was no time to ask. He dashed down to the dock and a few minutes later we heard the crash boat race out of the harbor.

Then a sub-chaser reported by radio that it had found the mysterious vessel and challenged her.

"Who is it?" Pierce asked.

"Don't know," said the sub-chaser. "They're using last month's identification signals."

The communications officer, who had just come in, said, "Blow them out of the water. They're supposed to keep up to date on identification signals."

Pierce considered the suggestion and rejected it. He told the sub-chaser, "Stay by the ship until daylight. Then escort her into the harbor."

By this time the anti-aircraft boys had gotten tired of waiting. One of them shot off a round. The others interpreted this as a signal to fire, and for a while the island was a very noisy place. The crew of a Liberty ship at the dock were confused by the excitement. Their captain was visiting ashore and the first mate, thinking the island was being invaded, ordered the men to cut the lines and get the ship away from the dock. Without tugs this attempt proved rash, and the ship slowly swung about and ran aground.

It was quite early the following morning when we watched an unusual convoy enter the harbor, preceded by Woodley's crash boat and two patrol crafts, and followed by three sub-chasers, the *Begonia* came steaming in at six knots and turned neatly to the dock after she passed the harbor net.

Woodley and I were in the captain's office when they brought Sergeant Kildon in. The captain looked tired. His eyes were blood-shot, his complexion splotched with red, and his breath strong.

"What the hell do you think you were doing?" the captain screamed at the sergeant.

Sergeant Kildon looked at him placidly. "I told them guys at Ogliuga they should of sent a dispatch," he said. Then he added, after a long minute, "Them guys just don't like to send dispatches."

Chapter 5

Naval Historical Center

Everyone liked Woodley, even Nooters. It must have been someone like Nooters that Abraham Lincoln had in mind when he said that you can fool some of the people all of the time. Nooters was a quartermaster third class who had been assigned to our office because no one else on the island needed another quartermaster. We didn't need one either. We had Warren, who did all our quartermastering in less than an hour a day.

When Nooters was assigned to our office, the commander told him to assist Warren. Since Warren had practically nothing to do, Nooter's duties remained for a long time undefined. Nooters was thirty-seven, a large awkward man with a narrow, wizened face and powerful hands. When he was given a tongue lashing by the commander, those hands opened and closed, opened and closed, and the veins puffed up. Once, when he was being ridiculed unfairly, I thought for a moment that he was going to pick up the commander and heave him through the window. It was a large window; it was open; and the commander would have fitted through it neatly. But Nooters controlled himself, and after he left the room I closed the window reluctantly.

Nooters told us that he had been a farmer in Arkansas, that he liked to work with his hands, that he had finished six grades in grammar school, and that he had eight children. He never did understand why he was in the navy; when he was drafted he had expressed a preference for the transportation corps in the army. Nor did he understand why he had been made a quartermaster. We didn't either.

Nooters complicated things almost immediately. He was not a man to whom you could convey ideas indirectly. Whenever the captain came into our office, for example, everyone managed to look busy. The commander was writing a report; Dutton was plotting courses on graph paper; I was phoning people about cargoes; Woodley was looking at a pamphlet on crash boats; Manley was typing; and Warren was filing official-looking documents. Only Nooters was sitting around, patently doing nothing.

We all jumped to our feet when the captain came in, assumed expressions of sober alertness, and returned energetically to our work when he murmured permission to carry on. Nooters was still sitting, looking at the captain with the idle curiosity of a friendly puppy. The captain walked over to him.

"Stand up," he ordered.

Nooters jumped up and saluted. The captain returned the salute automatically, then said, "What the hell is the matter with you? Don't you know you're not supposed to salute indoors?"

"Yes, sir," said Nooters, slightly rattled, and saluted again.

The captain's hand started to return the salute, paused, then dropped slowly to his side. He looked at Nooters for a long time, then he looked suspiciously at each of us. We were all concentrating on our jobs. The captain turned and walked out slowly, his dignified steps wobbling a little as he proceeded down the hall.

Considerable time passed before he visited us again.

After this incident the commander moved Nooters into the ship-plot room next door, where he would be concealed from unexpected visitors. Nooter's job now was to move the little discs on the wall chart every four hours. The discs, called pips, represented ships at sea in the Aleutians. Theoretically, by looking at the large wall chart to which the magnetized pips stuck, one could see at a glance where all the shipping was. Before Nooters came the system worked, but during his incumbency we ran into difficulties.

On the very first day, for example, Woodley noticed that the ships enroute to Adak were moving more rapidly than usual and asked Nooters about it. Nooters explained that it was quite all right. Pip number one was a destroyer making sixteen knots. Nooters had calculated, proudly, that this amounted to sixty-four knots for the four-hour period. So he moved pip number one a distance of sixty-four miles; then he moved each of the other pips the same distance.

"Nooters," Woodley said patiently, "Pip number two stands for the *Diamond Nut*, an old Alaskan freighter. She can't make more than eight knots, even with a tail wind. Her average speed is six knots. You shouldn't move her pip sixty-four miles in four hours."

"I shouldn't, sir?" Nooters asked.

"No," Woodley said.

"How much should I move it?"

"Try moving it just twenty-four miles."

"Yes, sir," Nooters agreed cheerfully. "I'll do that. Thanks very much, sir. You betcha."

Woodley went back to his desk. The commander used to get irritated at Nooters' adding "you betcha" to his replies. He thought it was unmilitary. But Woodley and I realized that Nooters intended it only as an expression of enthusiasm. There weren't many things he understood clearly, or even felt that he understood clearly. He liked to intensify those brief happy moments.

Nooters had been in the ship-plot room a week when I came in to locate a ship called the *Sacajawea*. I couldn't find any pip for the *Sacajawea* on the board, although it was listed in Nooter's log. I asked him why the ship wasn't being plotted.

He mumbled something. I said sternly, "Nooters, why isn't the *Sacajawea* on the board?"

"I run out of pips," he grumbled.

I was surprised. It was true that the twenty red pips were all being used, but he also had twenty white ones on his desk.

"Why don't you use one of these white pips?" I asked.

Again he hesitated. "I don't like to use them white ones," he finally admitted. "They ain't as pretty as the red ones."

To protect Nooters I instructed the man who relieved him to check Nooters' work carefully and correct his mistakes. Beldoni was very cooperative. He was an energetic young man, a signalman. Although there was a shortage of good signalmen in the navy at that time, we had a few extra ones on the base. I once asked the personnel officer why he kept these men when we didn't need them.

"It's not that simple," Rivers explained. "We do have more signalmen than we need, but we're short of stewards and electricians. If I can make a deal with the district personnel office, I'll trade. But if I just tell them I've got too many signalmen they'll take them away and I'll be short in my total complement." He looked at me, somewhat irritated. "It isn't simple."

So we used Beldoni in the ship-plot room to push pips. It took him ten minutes to change the positions of the ships at the beginning of his watch, and another ten minutes in the middle of it. The rest of the time he studied Spanish. He was convinced that after the war there would be great opportunities for Americans who spoke Spanish. All of South America was looking for American who spoke Spanish, he told me.

Beldoni didn't mind correcting Nooters' mistakes. Nooters kept pushing pips forward during the day and Beldoni kept pushing them back at night and there was no harm done. When the air force or the army or the admiral called to ask where a ship was, we gave its "approximate" position. We told the army and the air force that tides, currents, winds, and sea conditions made exact plotting impossible. We did not tell that to the admiral.

When a ship arrived ahead of schedule, Nooters always accounted for it by a tail wind. "Yes, sir, lieutenant," he told me, "that sure was a strong tail wind that pushed the *Partridge* here ahead of time. You betcha."

I nodded amiably and he went back into ship-plot, very pleased with himself. Once, when a ship came in earlier than expected, the commander called him in.

"Nooters," he said, "why is the *Henry Failing* here ahead of time? According to your plotting she isn't due until tonight."

"She had a strong tail wind, sir," Nooters said.

The commander was startled. "What are you talking about, Nooters? The *Failing* came from the east and we've had a west wind for two days. What the hell do you mean by a tail wind?"

Nooters looked unhappy and started to salute. He had a powerful urge to salute whenever he was disconcerted. The commander raised his hands. "Get out of here," he shouted. "Don't salute. Just get back in that room and stay there."

The commander stalked out. As Nooters walked slowly past my desk he mumbled to himself, "I'll bet he don't know what a tail wind is either."

As long as Beldoni followed Nooters in the ship-plot room, the board was fairly accurate, but when the new executive officer reorganized the watch schedule, we lost all control. The new officer was Lieutenant Commander Henry, whose family manufactured a famous American cigar. Having been commissioned from civilian life, he had had no sea duty before coming to Adak.

When Henry arrived on the island in a shiny new bridge coat with gleaming gold buttons, he was visibly upset. His was the only bridge coat on Adak; everyone else wore shapeless, dirty, warm parkas. Henry ordered all officers to wear their insignia on the shoulders of their parkas. He claimed that the lack of saluting in the Aleutians was due to the fact that it was impossible to distinguish, among hundreds of identical parkas, the officers from the enlisted men and the senior officers from the juniors. Henry wore extra large gold leaves on his coat and announced that henceforth navy officers would be permitted to use army insignia, which were twice as large.

His second order dealt with what he called the miserable state of the island's defenses. By that time, the war had moved far west of the Aleutians, and there had been no enemy planes or submarines near Adak for almost a year. Nevertheless, Henry organized an emergency defense corps to help the army defend Adak, should the need arise. The army had already decided that a Japanese attack was so unlikely that it had cut its complement to a small fraction of the original strength. But Henry made a survey of all the jobs on the base and then decreed that ten per cent of all navy personnel be assigned to a special defense corps.

We sent Beldoni to the corps, partly because he wanted to work out-of-doors and partly because Woodley was afraid of what might happen to Nooters on a new job.

The mix-up in the ship-plot room came as a result of Henry's third order, the most ridiculous of all. Before his arrival we used the conventional civilian schedule, working from eight to six every day. But Henry discovered, in a book on naval customs, that the standard naval work period was four hours at a time. He was unable to change the daytime routine; the captain forbade it in profane, vigorous, and unmistakable language. So Henry set up a new series of four-hour night watches that every officer on the base, except department heads, now had to stand in addition to his regular work.

Nobody except Henry ever believed that these extra watches served any useful purpose. We had previously become accustomed, once a month, to relieve Krueger as officer of the deck at 6:00 P.M. We would sit in his little office in the administration building during the evening and sleep on a cot next to the office that night. There was little to do on the O.O.D. watch except write "all secure" in the log every hour. We didn't really mind this break in the monotony, a leisurely assignment, restricting but dignified. One was sometimes entrusted with such tasks as phoning the captain and saying, "This is the officer of the deck, captain. You left word to be called at 0700. It is now 0700. Yes, sir. Thank you, sir." It wasn't too different from the watch Woodley and I had stood in the mess hall of the indoctrination school.

Lieutenant Commander Henry changed this casual arrangement. He divided the O.O.D. relief watch into four, four-hour periods. Krueger now went off duty at 1600 instead of 1800. Since at Adak the major difference between being O.O.D.-on-duty and O.O.D.-off duty consisted of changing one's location, Krueger was a little confused at first and tended to answer phones wherever he happened to be between 1600 and 1800.

In addition to creating four new night watches for the officer of the deck, Henry also divided the remainder of Nooter's ship-plot time into four extra watches and demanded that a different officer stand each of these watches.

This rearrangement made it necessary for Nooters to go to his hut two hours earlier than he had been accustomed to, a change that disturbed him even more than it did Krueger.

"I don't have nothing to do at the hut," Nooters protested. "Pierce ain't in the office much after four. I'll stay here."

"I'm sorry," I explained gently. "You have to go when you're relieved. You have to leave the ship-plot room."

Nooters looked at me resentfully. He associated all commands with the person transmitting them to him. I don't think it every occurred to him that orders might be conveyed through an intermediary. This accounted, I suspect, for his strong affection for the cooks and stewards; he felt they were indulging in a friendly personal gesture when they gave him meals, and he defended them vigorously when other men complained about the food.

Henry's reorganization of watches in the ship-plot room now made four officers do a job that had been done by one signalman. It made four more officers stand the O.O.D. watch that one officer stood previously. Now that there were eight times as many assignments as there had been before, each of us had to stand an extra watch every four days.

This was a hectic period in our Aleutian adventure. A half-hour before midnight, the officer of the deck sent his driver to get that driver's relief. (The drivers too were now on four-hour watches.) The driver stumbled around in three or four enlisted men's huts, waking a number of irritated men before he found the right one. The relief driver then drove to the officers' quarters and stumbled around in three or four officers' barracks, waking a number of furious officers before he found the one who had to relieve the O.O.D. The relief-O.O.D. and the relief driver then looked for the barracks of the officer who had to relieve the ship-plot man. When they found and awakened him they drove to the port building. The new officer of the deck then relieved the old officer of the deck, and the new ship-plot man relieved the old ship-plot man.

According to the instruction sheet we had been given at indoctrination school, the proper procedure at this point would have been to say, "Lieutenant Woodley reporting. I relieve you, sir." What usually was mumbled instead was "Hi, Mac. What's up?" There was rarely anything up. The two officers who had just arrived sat down in their respective offices, twenty feet apart, to spend the next four hours in any way except sleeping. The new driver drove the relieved officers back to their barracks, then came back to the port building to sit and kill time until 0330. At that time he would stumble into a few enlisted men's huts until he found the driver who was supposed to relieve him. The latest driver would then go up to the officers' quarters, find two more sleepy officers, and bring them down to the port building for a four-hour stint.

If Nooters was unhappy about being sent to his hut earlier than he had become accustomed to, he was even more unhappy over the things that happened in the ship-plot room during his absence. The men who now operated the ship-plot knew even less about it than he did. They were more intelligent than he was and could easily have learned to do the job if they wanted to. But since they were engineering officers, or personnel officers, or gunnery officers, who had already put in a day's work and viewed Henry's innovations with open contempt, they were careless in plotting ships. We soon realized that for purposes of accuracy we would have to keep our own records of ships' movements.

During this period Nooters craved companionship. The moment Pierce stepped out of the office, Nooters came in. Manley, Warren, and Mason stopped writing letters, lighted cigarettes, and gossiped. Warren announced the names of actresses who had recently sent him photographs. Manley speculated on possible ways of getting emergency leave: his wife had stopped writing to him altogether. And Nooters talked about his home in a small Arkansas town.

"How much rent do you pay?" Mason asked.

"Ten dollars a month," Nooters said. "Big house. Four bedrooms. I shoulda bought it before the war. The landlord asked four hundred bucks. He wants seven hundred now."

"Isn't your wife worn out, having eight children?" Warren teased him.

"No," Nooters said earnestly. "It gets easier all the time. Took her four hours with the first one. Last time she thought she had a stomachache and went out to the privy. The twins came right there."

Someone whispered, "Commander's coming," and Nooters scampered back to his room. He was afraid of Pierce and Pierce knew it. The commander knew whom he could bully and whom he couldn't, and it wasn't just a matter of rank. There were some enlisted men whom he treated courteously and whose explanations he accepted. Other he excoriated. When in doubt, he kept his temper.

His browbeating finally wore Nooters down. Nooters came into the office one day, marched up to the commander's desk, saluted, and said hurriedly, "Sir, I request a change of duty."

Pierce looked at him coldly. "What kind of duty do you want?"

"Any kind," said Nooters, staring straight

ahead of him, his arms stiff at his sides.

"Would you like sea duty?"

"Yes, sir."

The commander snorted. "What the hell could you do aboard ship? You'd drive a canoe on the rocks in five minutes. By God, you'll learn to do something right before I let you out of here. Now get back to your room and don't bother me."

Nooters stood there, clenching and unclenching his big hands. Then he turned and went back to his room. He didn't salute this time.

When I was censoring the mail the next day I found a bulky letter from Nooters to his wife. Usually Nooters couldn't fill up a single sheet of stationary, but this letter consisted of four pages. He ordered his wife to write to the Red Cross and ask them to get him sent home as a hardship case. She was to get her doctor to testify that she was working too hard and would collapse if she didn't get help. Nooters' final desperate supplication, repeated and underlined, was, "Tell the doc anything you want but get me outa here."

I sealed the letter and mailed it. The next day I had to read another thick letter to his wife. This one begged her to take immediate action on the subject of the previous day's letter. The subject was not directly referred to, but for a week Nooters wrote daily letters imploring his wife to take the necessary steps.

After that he watched the incoming mail eagerly, then broodingly. His letter writing fell off to the usual brief notes. A month later I read a postscript in one of his letters: "Please send me all the newspaper stories that say the war will soon be over."

The war ended today, and Nooters wore all of his campaign ribbons out there, posing for the photographers who arranged the fake celebration.

Chapter 6

It was Nooters who first told me that Woodley had been in an airplane crash. Nooters had been visiting the communications office when the news came in, and he immediately ran to our office and informed us. I asked Edwards to keep an eye on my desk, borrowed a jeep, and rushed over to the army hospital. There were a few soldiers standing around, but they weren't sure what had happened. A plane had crashed when landing; all of the occupants were now in the hospital. They were all dead, one man told me.

I hurried into the hospital and finally located the doctor in charge, a major. "It's the strangest damn thing I've ever seen," he said haltingly.

"The plane was smashed up and you'd expect them all to be killed. Three of them were. But a fourth guy is just shaken up a little. You can come in and see him if you want to."

I went into the room and saw Woodley lying on a bed, smiling weakly at me. He sat up and raised his hand in a mock salute.

"Are you all right?" I asked.

"I'm fine," he said. "I don't belong here. How are the other boys?"

The doctor shook his head. "They didn't make it. You're damned lucky you did. How did it happen?"

Woodley frowned. "I'd gone up with the boys on a reconnaissance flight. Routine stuff. Suddenly the fog came in fast. The zoomie thought he could make it and tried to land. Next thing I know we bang into the runway. I bounced up and down a couple of times, and then somebody pulled me out."

The doctor looked at him carefully. "Anything hurting you?"

Woodley stretched his legs, then his arms. "No," he said. "I'm fine. Can I get out of here now?"

"Better stay here tonight. I'll let you go in the morning if you feel all right."

The doctor looked at Woodley again, shook his head, and went out.

Woodley said he'd call me in the morning when he was ready to be picked up, and I went back to the office.

The next day Woodley took it easy at his desk. At four o'clock he asked whether I'd like to take a ride to the salmon creek with him, and we came out here and walked up to the spot where we're sitting now. It was a couple of months ago, and the salmon weren't running, but everything else was just about the same. There were these beautiful flowers that don't give off any odor, and the seagulls were diving, and the snowline on the mountains was a little higher. We sat here on the tundra and talked. Our voices sounded louder than they were because there aren't any other sounds here.

"I don't have to tell you how glad we are that you're all right," I said.

"Why, were you boys worried about me?"

"Of course we were worried," I said. "Weren't you?"

"No."

I stared at him. "Oh, come on, Pete. What do you mean you weren't worried?"

He spoke very earnestly. "I don't want you to misunderstand, Jack. But I told you once before. I'm being saved for some special purpose—and I'm not going to be killed off before that purpose is accomplished."

"What is this purpose?"

"I haven't any idea. My mother is sure God has some great religious work for me to do. But I honestly don't know. I told you I was saved when my grammar school burned. I was saved when my canoe tipped over. And I was saved yesterday when the plane crashed. I can't tell you how I know, but I want you to believe me. I wasn't afraid yesterday—I knew I was safe."

We didn't say anything for a long time. It was quiet and lovely and peaceful. Woodley stretched and looked out at the tundra.

"Not even one tree here," he said. "On the whole island. Not even a bush."

"The Seabees built a tree," I said. "It's the only one in the Aleutians. They put a big sign in front of it, announcing the fact."

Woodley looked off across the bay. "That's one of the big things on my list when I get back to the States. Look at trees. Millions of them."

"What else is on your list?"

"Oh, the usual things. A comfortable hotel room, sleeping late, fresh milk and avocado salad, and crowds and buildings and women walking around. God, lots of things."

"And?"

"Oh, I want to see my mother, of course. I'm an only child; Dad died when I was seven. Mother centered her life about me. She's the one who first realized that I've been miraculously saved. After that school fire, she kept saying, ''Twas the Lord's mercy.' The parents of the dead kids didn't like it, but they never said anything to me about it. And after the canoe business, some other people in the neighborhood came around to feeling the way Mother did. I don't know, it wouldn't make sense to save me twice—three times, now—for nothing."

I lit a cigarette. "Anything else you looking forward to in the States?"

He grinned. "There sure is. I'm going to look up Eva when I get back."

"Eva? Oh, the girl on the train. You still hear from her?"

He took a couple of pink envelopes out of his pocket and patted them. "I sure do. She's done a lot of traveling since I met her. The USO really gets around. I wish they'd get up here. She's a sweet kid."

I remembered the episode with Merkle, but I didn't say anything.

"She hopes to open a dancing school after the war. For children. She says nobody in her family ever did anything but farming or factory work, and she is going to be more important than that. She wants her mother to be proud of her, and she's saving her money. Here's a picture she sent me." Woodley took a snapshot out of his wallet. "It's not too good a likeness, you remember what a pretty girl she is, but I'm glad she sent it. She promised me that if her troupe ever gets up to the Aleutians, I've got a date with her the first night."

"I'm sure you'll enjoy it," I said.

Woodley smiled. "Remember Dutton saying there's nothing in the world you can catch up on as fast as sex? There are a lot of other things in life. I like to see people having fun, and I want to play football and sail and see the country. I've got so much energy saved up I'm going to have an awfully good time for a long time after the war is over."

"I hope you have it," I said. "I hope you're not disappointed."

He laughed. "Don't talk like an old man, Jack. Your only thirty."

"It's not the age," I said. "On my last leave I took my four-year-old nephew to the circus. He had a wonderful time. I hadn't been to a circus for a long time, and I looked forward to it. But I was very disappointed. The acrobats seemed fat and awkward, the clowns were childish, and the animals were shabby. The sugar candy tasted flat, and the red drinks were just ice with a vile flavor. Even the barker sounded like a parody of all barkers. I found it hard to believe that anyone enjoyed it."

"But the kids enjoyed it," Woodley said.

"Oh, yes. My nephew was fascinated."

"I'm like your nephew," Woodley said. "I still enjoy things. I get a kick out of lots of things.

I'm happy just being young and healthy, and I've got a lot of strong, simple desires to satisfy. The war will be over soon. I'll have a long time to make up for these two years in the Aleutians."

"It's good to feel that way," I said.

He was quiet for a while, looking at the jagged line of mountains in the distance. "I don't always feel this way," he said quietly.

I waited, and he was silent for a long time. Then he went on. "I went home before shipping out. It was nice being with Mother and old friends. Then I felt depressed about going overseas and leaving people who really cared about me. Don't get me wrong—I wasn't afraid. Even if I weren't sure there's a purpose in my life, I wouldn't have been afraid of going to the Aleutians. There's less chance of getting killed here than in big city traffic. But I was sort of melancholy, so I went over to the old high school."

Woodley looked off into space again, into the fog that was quickly dropping around us. We could not see the mountains any more. "I'd been pretty important at the high school," he said. "I'd been football captain and I had played baseball and basketball just a few years before. So I stood around, trying to recapture the feeling of satisfaction and security that I used to have. But the kids at school didn't know me, and nobody said anything to me. I stood watching them chatter and fool around, and I felt alone and lonesome and outside of it all. I wanted very much to be part of something permanent, something that had been there and would keep on being there. But it wasn't there any more."

Woodley laughed, a little sadly. "So I went home and ate a big steak and forgot about it. And I haven't felt that way since. Except maybe once or twice."

We walked down along the creek. The fog had dropped almost to ground level, and we drove slowly back to the officers' quarters. When we got into the dining room, most of the men had already eaten and we took an empty table.

"Look at Rogers," Woodley said.

I watched Rogers stop in the doorway, look around the room imperiously, and step in. Rogers was a slim, handsome twenty-two year old who had just become a lieutenant (junior grade) because an all-navy order automatically promoted all ensigns who had served fifteen months.

His transformation was startling. For fifteen months he had begun telephone conversations by saying "Rogers talking." The day after his promotion, and from then on, the phrase was changed to "Lieutenant Rogers speaking." Most men made the necessary alterations in uniform after being promoted but Rogers, it appeared, had had new gray and blue uniforms shipped from the States long before. The stripe and a half on his cuff was clearly new braid—not, as in the case of less eager officers, a bright half-stripe added to a faded full one.

We usually did our work in old trousers and open shirts but Rogers, from the day of his promotion, wore a complete uniform to work and meals. He cultivated an expression of frowning concentration, looking off into space, obviously thinking out problems beyond the scope of his companions. I watched him now, as he entered the room like a man singularly conscious of the fact that he is entering a room. He walked by our table and Woodley caught his eye.

"Good evening, lieutenant," Woodley said.

"Good evening, sir," Rogers said and walked on. Junior officers were not in the habit of addressing each other as "sir," and a month before he had called Woodley "Pete." He took a table by himself, pounded noisily for the steward, and ordered dinner.

"Funny guy," Woodley said. "And still on the same job."

When the base had first been set up in preparation for the assaults on Attu and Kiska, the navy complement had been much larger. At that time the executive officer, a captain, had been assigned an aide. Since then the size of the navy establishment had shrunk considerably and the rank of the present executive officer was only lieutenant commander, but the job of aide still existed. There wasn't much for the captain to do, or for the executive officer; there was less for the captain's aide; and there was practically nothing for the executive officer's aide.

Rogers was the exec's aide. He opened the mail in the morning; he took messages for the exec; and he answered the phone, since his promotion, with "Lieutenant Rogers speaking."

Aldrich came in and sat down at our table. He was the visual aids officer and was often teased about his educational films. The men, knowing that the Aleutian waters could freeze them to death in ten minutes, showed little interest in movies teaching swimming. Nor was there much point in teaching lookout procedure to men who were permanently fog bound. (One merchant captain had told me that in three years of Aleutian sailing he had never seen the chain of islands; he sailed entirely by instrument.) And there was some doubt about the wisdom of showing a venereal disease film on an island without women.

"What kept you so late?" Woodley asked.

"That damn VD movie again," Aldrich said. "If we run it once we run it three times a day. There's one machinist's mate that must have seen it a hundred times. He knocks off work at 1700 and catches the 1730 show every day."

While we were eating, Ensign Rigler came in. He stood in the entranceway and looked around the room apprehensively. Aldrich whispered, "Rigler's been acting peculiar lately."

The steward led Rigler over to our table. He sat down without looking at any of us and stared at his plate. Rigler was assistant issuing officer. The issuing office distributed the classified publications, and Rigler corrected and kept up to date the navy codes, pamphlets, and books. According to navy regulations he could be court-martialed if he made a mistake. Most issuing officers took their jobs in stride after a while, but Rigler seemed more and more disturbed by his duties and had lately been going to the office evenings to recheck the day's work.

"What's new?" Aldrich asked him.

Rigler raised his head slowly, looked at us vacantly, then stared at his plate again. We continued the meal in silence. Rigler ate mechanically, then stopped, looked at the meat, potatoes, and beans on his plate, gently picked up the plate, and turned it over on his head. Then he smiled at us pleasantly.

He didn't resist when we took him to the hospital.

It was nine o'clock then but still quite light. It would stay light for another hour, then the clouds would turn black. There would be no moon and no stars. We had not seen them often since we had arrived on Adak. We looked eastward toward the volcano on the next island but could not see it. Three thousand miles beyond it, in the States, it was now one o'clock in the morning. It seemed a long way and a long time.

Chapter 7

The following morning Mason reminded me that Woodley and I were scheduled to make inspections. Woodley had a few things to take care of at the dock first, and while I waited for him I looked through the outgoing mail, which I was supposed to censor. It was my job to make sure that no military information got out of our building. Since the security officer had ruled that no reference to the weather in the Aleutians was permitted, the material for casual chitchat in letters was rather limited. The island was geologically interesting, but its terrain was a military secret. The advance of the snowline down the mountainside as winter approached was a topic of daily conversation but forbidden in letters. The security officer's reasoning in this instance was frequently quoted, especially at the bar. "Snow is part of the weather," Lieutenant Bates had ruled, "and, by God, you're not going to write about the weather."

The letters varied in literary effect. Every week one boatswain's mate clumsily printed the same letter, word for word, to his mother. He told her that he was well, that he hoped she was well, and that he looked forward to seeing her when the war was over. A somewhat different kind of correspondent was the electrician's mate, who wrote to four women regularly, beginning each letter with "My own beloved darling." One of the four was his wife. A young seaman in Woodley's crash boat was consistent in still another way. He always ended his daily letter to his wife with "Yours in Christ." And Warren enclosed a stick of chewing gum in every letter he sent to his girl friends.

In most of the letters the themes were simple. The men expressed their hope for peace, home, and work. The three thousand miles between the Aleutians and the men's homes invested the latter with considerable charm. The wives were lovely, the children adorable, and the houses beautiful. Although in daily conversations the men talked a lot about their plans for catching up on sexual activities, in letters little of the fervor appeared. Leaders of nations orated about inevitable destinies, but the men in Adak dreamed of wives and girls and comfort. They had no more interest in economics or politics or philosophy than when they had left home. They doubted that the world would be any better when they had won the war, and they hoped that it wouldn't be worse.

Laboriously they wrote letters and watched the skies carefully when the mail plane was expected. As the four-engine transport glided toward a landing, most of the eyes on the island followed it. Everyone calculated how long it would be before the mail was sorted. Long before that time, each department had found an excuse to send a messenger to the post office, where he waited in a long line for the sacks to be emptied and filing completed.

One evening when Woodley and I drove down to the post office, a young sailor who had been loitering near the door came up to us hesitantly.

"What is it?" asked Woodley.

"Please, sir," the boy said. "Could you see if there's a letter for me."

"The last mail call was at five o'clock."

"Yes, sir. I didn't get any mail at five. I thought some mail came in since then."

Woodley knew, and the boy knew, that there had been no mail plane that evening, but he asked the boy's name and looked in the box. There was no mail.

"Thank you, sir," the boy said. "I thought there might be."

He walked slowly up the hill, his hands in his pockets, an unmilitary posture that the executive officer would have criticized severely.

Mason reminded me again that it was inspection time, so I put aside the rest of the mail and we went to the dock to get Woodley. Then we marched into the officer-of-the-deck's room. Krueger was reading a magazine.

Mason called out, "Inspection party," and Krueger sat up quickly, slipped the magazine under a blotter, and looked up.

"Oh, it's you," he said, and pulled the magazine out again. "What's up?"

"Woodley and I have inspection duty," I said. "Any special place we're suppose to check on?"

Krueger looked through some records. "You might go to the recreation building. There've been complaints about it in some of the inspection reports. Go see how old Toomley is doing."

Krueger grinned. Lieutenant Toomley was a fidgety, incompetent officer who had been shifted from one job on the island to another in the attempt to find the spot where he could do the least harm. Now he was the assistant recreation officer, in charge of distributing tickets to local entertainments and giving toothpaste samples to newly arrived seamen.

We drove over to the recreation building. Mason walked into Toomley's office ahead of us and shouted, "Inspection party. Attention!" Mason liked going on inspections. We went in and watched Toomley scramble to his feet. He had been lying back in a lounge chair, reading; his tie and belt were loose, but he jumped to attention. Toomley was senior to both of us, but he never felt sure enough of himself to relax on what he felt was an official occasion. We stopped in front of him and looked him up and down, trying not to smile. Toomley stared straight ahead.

I looked at the paper on the floor. "The deck is dirty," I said.

Toomley's eyes skittered frantically down, then back. "I told the yeoman to clean it up—forgot about inspection day—meant to . . . ."

I couldn't keep a straight face, so I looked at the wall, which was streaked with dust. "The bulkheads need cleaning," I said.

"Yes, sir," said Toomley. He didn't really have to say "sir."

"Where is your yeoman?" Woodley asked.

Toomley looked unhappy. "I don't know. He's never around when I want him. I told him to stay here and he said he would be right back and— " Toomley waved his hands helplessly. "I don't know where he is."

I looked at him and grinned. He smiled back timidly. "OK," I said. "See you at lunch."

Mason followed us out in the hall. "What do I write in the report?" he asked.

Woodley and I looked at each other and laughed. We had both been reprimanded in the past for failure to use proper nautical language in reports. Once Commander Henry had rebuked me for not calling the library window a "port." And Woodley had been criticized for saying that the ceiling in the recreation room was cracked; he should have called it the "overhead."

"The hell with it," Woodley told Mason. "Write that everything was ship-shape." Mason frowned and wrote something in his notebook. Next we drove to one of the enlisted men's huts and inspected it. It was clean and neat, although a purist might have felt that there was an excessive amount of female anatomy displayed on the walls. Over one bed were crowded the best of the bulging pinups from *Newsweek*. Another seaman obviously favored buttocks: the space by his bed was covered with cutouts of pants, girdles, and similar lingerie from Sears and Montgomery Ward catalogues. His neighbor seemed to specialize in breasts and had accumulated an impressive collection of brassiere ads from women's magazines and nudes from less reputable sources. Woodley told Mason that we had no criticism to put in the report, and we drove back to the office.

After lunch the captain called with news of an unexpected break in routine. He wanted Woodley to get together with Tom Belding, the harbormaster, and entertain a group of Russian naval officers that evening. The captain would take care of the high-ranking officers himself, but he expected Woodley and Belding to arrange something for the others. Woodley agreed enthusiastically and went off to the harbormaster's office to talk to Belding.

Russian ships did not ordinarily stop at Adak. They sailed through Japanese waters from Vladivostok to Kamchatka, and thence through American seas to Portland. They carried supplies for Americans to use against Japan, and the Japanese exercised notable restraint in escorting these semi-neutral ships to a place where Americans could assume responsibility for their safe passage. We routed the Russians a hundred miles north of the Aleutians to maintain our own security.

When the *Nicolai Kuznitzoff* broke in two, we had to sacrifice security for hospitality. Our tugs towed the halves of the unfortunate ship to an island near Adak and provided facilities for the enlisted men there. But diplomacy required that the officers be brought to Adak for a friendly visit, and Woodley and Belding were assigned to entertain them.

Belding was a tough, independent pilot who didn't worry much about superiors or subordinates. He piloted ships; he ran the harbor; and he passed all correspondence to his yeoman with the ambiguous command, "Take care of this junk for me."

Belding and Woodley decided to give a party at Belding's Quonset and to invite Krueger, Bates, and me. Bates, the security officer, had volunteered to serve as interpreter. We met the four Russians at Belding's hut after work, and Bates introduced them as Sonovich, Sonomich, Sonobich, and Sonotich. When Woodley said he was surprised at the similarity in names, Bates explained that the "Son" root was very common in Russian names. The Russians seemed puzzled, in spite of Bates's vigorous jabbering to them.

Belding told me, "I should never have invited that bastard Bates. He's bluffing. He doesn't know a word of Russian. I'm going to call Jack Malley."

When Malley, the admiral's intelligence officer, arrived he explained to the Russians that Bates was drunk and reintroduced them as Shostapol, Bubof, Aleskov, and Shenko. In the dining room, where Woodley had reserved a table, our guests disposed enthusiastically of mushroom soup, fried chicken, sweet potatoes, peas, fresh tomatoes, apple pie, and coffee. After dinner we took them to the theater. The enlisted men were waiting in line outside. Malley asked whether there was any discrimination between officers and enlisted men in the Russian navy. Aleshkov smiled wryly and said something. Malley translated, "He says it's about the same, but there are fewer movies in Russia."

After the movie we went back to Belding's hut and talked and drank. Our guests relaxed gradually, all except Bubof, who sat straight in his chair, drinking slowly and consistently and nodding politely but aloofly.

Woodley and Shenko were playing checkers, studying their moves very deliberately, when we heard a loud noise. It was Bates falling down drunk. The men rolled him against the wall and began to play darts. Belding, Bubof, Aleshkov, and Shestopol took turns throwing darts at the cardboard target on Belding's closet door. After a while Aleshkov put down the darts, took out his big sailor's knife, and threw that. Bubof and Belding approved the innovation, found knives, and threw them for a while. Shostapol finished his bottle, shrieked happily, and started shooting at the target with his pistol. He shot from where he sat, and Bubof and Aleshkov shot from where they stood.

"You guys can't even shoot straight," Belding shouted. They nodded affably. Belding went to his bedroom, got out his revolver, lined up with the Russians, and took his turn shooting at the target. His aim was not much better than theirs.

At two o'clock we ran out of liquor and ammunition. Bates had revived and was telling one of his interminable stories about people who had mistreated him. "So this damn Jones told me to get off his ship and stay off. How do you like that?" He grumbled unintelligibly, then said, "Where the hell is Jones's ship now?"

"It's on patrol in the outer harbor," Woodley said.

Bates took Woodley aside and talked to him. Woodley seemed to disagree at first, then he laughed and turned to us. "Come on. We're going to pep up this party."

The Russians put away their guns and we all piled into two jeeps and went down to the port office. We waited there while Woodley and Bates drove off. They returned with a sleepy and puzzled Chinese sailor. Wong, the captain's mess boy, was popular because of his baking and his accent. Woodley explained to Wong what he wanted.

Every hour the ship out on patrol reported to the port office on short wave radio. The officer on the ship would call in, "Green calling Red. Green calling Red. Over."

The port office spokesman would reply, "Red calling Green. Proceed. Over."

The ship would then say, "Green calling Red. All secure. Over."

The port officer would respond with "Red to Green. Over. Roger and out," and the ship would conclude with "Green to Red. Roger, out."

At 0300 Wong, the Russians, and the rest of us gathered around the port office radio. The loudspeaker sputtered and we heard, "Green calling Red. Green calling Red. Over."

Woodley handed the microphone to Wong and whispered, "Go ahead." Wong took the mike and called out, "Led calling Glin. Led calling Glin. Ploceed. Ovah."

There was a long moment of silence, then the voice came through again, a little hesitantly. "Green calling Red. Green calling Red. Over."

Wong called back cheerfully. "Led calling Glin. Led calling Glin. Ploceed. Ovah."

This time the pause lasted much longer. The radio sputtered intermittently, then a new, excited voice broke in. "Red calling Green. Over."

Bates whispered happily, "That's Jones. That's the old son-of-a-bitch himself."

Wong said calmly, "Led calling Glin. Led calling Glin. Ploceed. Lodja. Ovah."

This time the radio vibrated. "What the hell is going on there?"

"Ploceed," said Wong. "Lodjah. Ovah."

There was no more sound from the radio. Five minutes later we saw the patrol ship, lit up, speed into the harbor, make a violent turn toward the dock, and approach it at a speed few captains would permit. A figure jumped off the ship before the lines were tied and a moment later a jeep raced toward the port office.

We waited, Bates beaming, Belding roaring, and the Russians smiling feebly. Jones ran into the port office, gun in hand. The sight of us casually sprawled out seemed to surprise him. He stared at Wong. Wong grinned cordially and said, "'Allo." Jones put his gun back in the holster, started to say something, then stopped. He turned around, went back to his jeep, and drove slowly back to the dock. Soon we saw the patrol vessel move away from the dock, turn, and sail leisurely out of the harbor.

We took the Russians back to their quarters. They didn't seem upset by the evening's activity. They did seem somewhat puzzled.

In the morning Belding came into the office fuming. "There are holes in all my clothes," he muttered angrily. "Pete, some son-of-a-bitch has been shooting up my clothes closet."

Chapter 8

For days after the trick on Lieutenant Jones, everyone in the office laughed and talked about the incident. Everyone but Manley, that is. Manley had been taking less and less part in the conversations and dragged himself around dispiritedly until Woodley took him down to the dock and had a talk with him. Manley's wife had stopped writing altogether; his mother was evasive in her letters; and the Red Cross had not found out anything for him. "Maybe they'll try harder if you say something to them, Mr. Woodley," Manley said.

Woodley promised to do what he could and that evening he asked me to go with him to the Red Cross office. Bob Saunders, the Red Cross director and a regular member of our poker club, had three men waiting to see him. He asked whether we were in a hurry. When we said that we weren't, he suggested that we wait in his private office. The partition in the office was placed at such an angle that we could see his visitors without being seen ourselves.

A husky, good-looking boy came in, smiled pleasantly, and told Saunders, "I got this letter today and I thought I'd show it to you."

Saunders read the letter aloud. "Dear Mr. Murray. Maybe you remember my daughter Shirley Korzybski. We live in Waukegan, Illinois. When you was at Great Lakes you took Shirley out lots of times. Once you ate supper here. Shirley is going to have a baby soon. If you like to marry her before baby born very nice. I thought you like to know about baby. She say it's your baby. Yours truly, Mrs. Stella Korzybski."

"Is she right about the baby?" Saunders asked.

Murray scratched his head. "I don't know. I was at Great Lakes all right. And there was a Polish girl I laid a couple of times. But I don't remember her name or what she looked like. I guess I'd know her again if I saw her."

"What do you want me to do about it?"

"I don't know. Do I have to marry her?"

"Probably not. Some other man may have been the father."

Murray grinned. "I get it. Yeh. She wasn't any virgin."

"Well?"

"I don't know. Maybe it is my kid. Could I get leave to get married?"

"We could try. It depends on the head of your division."

"Yeh," said Murray. "Now how about an allotment? If I married her, would they take it out of my pay or would they give me more money?"

"Probably both. The Navy would pay an allotment to your wife and child, and it would also deduct part of your pay."

"Well, there's one more thing I've got to figure. If I go back to the States to marry her, will the Navy send me back here after my leave is up?"

"How long have you been in the Aleutians?"

"Eight months."

"In that case," Saunders said, "There's a good chance that they won't send you back here."

Murray thought it over for a minute. "I'll tell you," he said, "I think I ought to marry that girl. I feel like I got—a—a . . ."

"Responsibility?"

"Yeh. I got a responsibility to the kid. Sure.

Will you get me leave?"

"I'll try," Saunders said. "I hope you and Miss—what's her name?"

Murray looked at the letter. "Korzybski. Shirley Korzybski."

"Yeh," Murray said. "We'll take care of it. Thanks a lot."

The next visitor was a lean, leather-faced man about forty, wearing dungarees. He told Saunders, rubbing his hands nervously while he talked, that he had just received a telegram. His father was ill and was not expected to live.

"Is there anyone with your father now?" Saunders asked.

"My brother is there."

Saunders shook his head. "To get emergency leave, you'd have to be the only person who could handle that particular problem. What could you do that your brother can't?"

The man shrugged. "I don't know. I'd like to see the old man."

The man walked out, rubbing his chin with his greasy hand.

Now a heavy-featured, slack-jawed young man shuffled into Saunders' office. He said hesitantly, "I'm John Glask. I drive for the central office."

He held out his hand. Saunders shook it.

"What can I do for you?"

"Can we talk in private?"

Saunders assured him that they could.

"OK," Glask said. "The chief said I oughta talk to you about it. He said you could do something about it."

"About what?"

"About my wife."

"What about her?"

"She's a very sexy woman," Glask said.

"Oh?"

"She gotta have it often," Glask explained.

"I see."

"I got a letter here from her," Glask said. "She wants me to come home and take care of her."

Saunders took the letter gingerly. "What do you expect me to do about it?"

Glask seemed surprised. "Why, the chief said you'd get me a furlough if I showed you that letter."

Saunders smiled faintly. "What do you expect me to tell the captain when he asks the reason for your furlough?"

"Put it real nice," Glask said. "The chief said you know what kind of words to use."

Saunders returned the letter. "I'm sorry. I'm afraid I can't help you. The chief was kidding you."

"No," Glask argued. "they all said I should go to the Red Cross."

"All? Who else?"

"The boys in the office and the boys in the hut. They all said I oughta come here."

"Do you mean you show your wife's letters to everybody?"

"Sure. She's got real nice handwriting. Look at it."

Saunders stood up. "It's very nice handwriting, but I can't help you." Then he said. "Tell me something. If you've been showing everybody the letters, why did you worry about talking to me in private?"

"Officers is different," Glask said and stood up.

Saunders walked with him to the door and said, "Ask the chief to help you."

"He'd like to but he can't," Glask said sadly as he walked out. "He's going back to the States next week."

Saunders joined us in his office and Woodley asked him about Manley. Saunders frowned. "It's a ticklish business," he said. "I feel sorry for the guy, but I haven't been able to do anything for him. Here is the story, although Manley doesn't know it. There was a man living with his wife for a while, but he moved out. Now she is rumored to be running around with another man, but we can't prove it. Without mentioning any names, I felt out Commander Pierce at the club the other day, and I got the impression that he wouldn't have much sympathy for an enlisted man in that situation. I don't think he would approve Manley's furlough request, so I've been holding it back until Pierce goes on leave. Pierce is giving his promotion party tonight, and he goes on leave Monday. Then we can try to get a furlough for Manley."

We agreed that that would be the best thing to do and went home to get dressed for Pierce's party.

Chapter 9

Pierce had reserved the entire navy club and invited every high-ranking officer on the island. A few men whose jobs were more important than their rank, and all the officers in his department, were also asked to attend. The steward said later that it was the most expensive party given on the base.

Promotions at Pierce's level were viewed more seriously than at ours. Ensigns and junior-grade lieutenants were eligible for automatic promotion by AlNav after they had completed fifteen months in one rank. Unless their commanding officer objected, they simply added another half stripe of gold braid to their uniforms. But to make full commander you had to put in at least two years of duty and be recommended by a committee in Washington. It was customary at such times to tell successful candidates that they fully deserved their promotion and to assure the others that someone in Washington was prejudiced.

When Woodley and I arrived, the party had been going on for some time. Usually the club opened at eight in the evening, but from seven-thirty on straggling individuals converged on it. Until the doors opened the men would stand around impatiently and grumble that making a man wait for his drink until eight o'clock was undemocratic, uncivilized, and unbearable. By the time the door opened a large number of habitués would be waiting to rush in.

Time dragged on in the Aleutians. You couldn't go hiking through the soggy tundra in fall and in spring, or in the snowdrifts in winter. The only women on the island were a dozen nurses, and there was nothing to do at night except sit in the hut, or go to the movies, or drink at the club. Some men went to the club every night.

Many of the men went to the theater, where a different picture was shown every evening. For ten cents an officer could go to the enormous elephant-hut, enter the reserved section without waiting in the long line of enlisted men, and see a movie in comfort. He could not, of course, sit in the front row of the officers' section, reserved for the captain and his party. Neither the captain nor his party attended the theater very often, but their seats remained reserved and unused. Some men went to the theater night after night, for fifteen or eighteen or twenty-four months, sat there all evening, and then went home to sleep in preparation for another day of work and another evening at the movies.

On the night of Pierce's party, we saw an indignant officer trying to get in and a patient chief petty officer keeping him out. The officer was small and the chief was large, and it seemed to me that the former was wasting his time.

He turned to us. "Did you hear the chief?" he wailed. "He says the club is reserved tonight."

"That's right," I said. "They're having a private party in there."

He shook his head sadly and turned again to the chief. "I don't get it. The whole goddamn club reserved. Look," he began, talking slowly, as if he were explaining something to a child, "I don't want to go to the party. I don't give a damn about the party. All I want is a drink. Every night I come here at this time; I walk in; I order a drink; I drink it. Get it? That's all I want."

We left him expostulating with the chief and went in. Commander Pierce, flushed and happy, met us at the door.

"Glad you could make it, boys," he told us. He put an arm around each of us and whispered, "The admiral may come. I didn't know whether I should invite him, but his aide said, 'Sure, why don't you ask him, he won't get mad,' so I mailed him an invitation and tonight I got word that the admiral will show up. Isn't that nice of him?"

We agreed that it was nice and gave the steward our orders. There was a lot of gold braid around, and the only seats we could find were at Captain Bard's table. Bard was an Annapolis man commanding a cruiser, a small bald man in his late fifties with a high voice that grew tinny as he drank. The others at the table were Bard's executive officer, a commander; Rivers, the personnel officer; Dutton, from our office; and a red-faced, glazed-eyed man whom I did not know.

The captain was saying, "So I told him that we regular navy men had no prejudice against the reserves at all. No prejudice in the world. None at all. I don't care what you hear about favoritism. I guess you won't hear that man complain any more. Well, anyhoo—"

He giggled and the commander chuckled.

"You're absolutely right," said Dutton.

"Yes, sir," said Rivers.

The red-faced man shifted his gaze slowly around the table and said, deliberately and distinctly, pronouncing each syllable carefully, "You're not kidding."

The captain took a drink, settled into a comfortable position, and said, "Mark my word, it's the navy that's winning the war. I was saying to Peterson Friday . . . let me see, was it Friday or Saturday? Peterson, when was it?"

"Friday, sir," the commander said.

"I was telling Peterson Friday," said the captain, "the navy is winning the war. Chester asked me once, 'How long do you think it will take?' and I told him, 'Admiral,' I said, 'the Golden Gate in forty-eight.' You mark my word. Well, anyhoo—"

He giggled. The commander chuckled.

"That certainly sounds right," said Dutton.

"Yes, sir," said Rivers.

"You're not kidding," the red-faced man said.

"I've been in the navy thirty-seven years," the captain said. "I'll tell you who makes the best officer. It's not the introvert, not your artist or dreamer. It's the salesman type. The guy who can sell you the Brooklyn Bridge. The guy who doesn't worry about theories but knows his job and does it. Without asking questions. That's the kind of officer I want. Anyhoo—"

He giggled. The commander laughed.

"I would certainly agree," said Dutton.

"Yes, sir," said Rivers.

The red-faced man stared steadily at the glass in front of him, trying to keep it from becoming two glasses. "You're not kidding," he said, very deliberately.

Someone called "Attention" and we all stood up. The captain raised himself reluctantly, and the red-faced man was able to stand only because Dutton and Rivers held him up. The admiral walked in, trailed by a retinue of captains and commanders. The two gold stripes above the solid gold bar on his sleeve made me think of a child dressed up for a masquerade. But the admiral clearly did not think of himself as a masquerader. He shook hands with the captains, then with the senior commanders, and finally with beaming, nervous Commander Pierce.

"Congratulations, commander," he said.

"Thank you very much, sir," said Pierce. "May I get you a drink?"

"Please do," said the admiral. Then he looked around the room and said, "Be seated, gentlemen."

Woodley walked over to the slot machine, put in a few dimes, and hit the small jackpot. It was the twenty-eighth of the month. We stuffed our pockets with dimes and sat down with a group that was listening to the senior medical officer.

"If I could set up a control group," the doctor was saying, "I'd prove my theory was right."

"What theory is that?" Woodley asked.

"We have a higher percentage of mental illness in the Aleutians than in any other non-combat zone in the world. Know why?" The doctor pounded the table. "It's the low barometric pressure here. Think a moment. Don't you feel depressed just before a storm?"

He looked at me severely and, to avoid arguing, I nodded. He looked at Woodley. Woodley hesitated, then said, "Sometimes." The doctor looked at Dutton.

"Yes, sir," said Dutton. "That's right."

"There you are," the doctor said. "It always feels here as if it's going to storm. It's no wonder people get nervous breakdowns."

Woodley and I flipped coins. I lost and went to the bar for more drinks. When I came back the doctor was saying, "Never performed so many adult circumcisions in my life. At least one a day. Wonderful experience."

The chaplain asked whether that was an unusual operation.

"No," the doctor said, "but it hurts. And you have to treat it gently for a long time after cutting."

Woodley smiled. "Adak's the perfect place to be circumcised, then."

"That's right," said the doctor. "Could I interest you, perhaps? It's a very simple operation."

"No, thanks," Woodley said hurriedly. "Not me. Tell us about your trip to Seattle last week, Doc."

The doctor was still looking speculatively at Woodley and changed the subject reluctantly.

"I had a good time, considering that it was emergency leave. Had some legal business to attend to. Those stateside medical officers have it easy, living like damned civilians, going to the hospital in the morning and home again at night. What do they know about war?"

The doctor looked at us belligerently and Dutton agreed that stateside doctors knew nothing about war. The doctor finished his drink and stared disconsolately into the empty glass. "They just don't understand," he muttered, more to himself than us. "That district officer tells me we've shipped too many mental cases to the States. The old fool. I have a man in the hospital now, blowing a saxophone. He's been blowing the damn thing for three days. Won't do anything else."

"What's wrong with him?" I asked.

"Oh, his girlfriend sent him a 'Dear John.' He asked for emergency leave but didn't get it. Electrician's mate. You can't let enlisted men go back to the States all the time, you know. You can understand that."

"Why is he playing a saxophone?" I asked.

"He used to play the sax when he was a boy. Won a high-school contest once," he said. The doctor stood up. "I guess I'll turn in now," he said in a tired voice. "I can't drink the way you young men do." He looked at Woodley. "You're sure you don't want to be circumcised? Very minor operation, you know. Nothing to it."

"No, sir," said Woodley emphatically.

"All right," said the doctor. "Good night, gentlemen. See you tomorrow."

He walked out and we talked for a while about stateside duty. "Those boys sure have it soft," Krueger said. "Just think of it, making the rounds at night, and women all over the place. Boy, what I could do to a woman tonight."

"You wouldn't know what to do if you got it on a silver platter," Bates said.

"I'd know what to do," Krueger said.

"Do all those guys stateside have a drag in Washington?" Dutton asked.

"You've got to know somebody in BuPers, Bates said. "If you get the right connection in BuPers, they'll never send you overseas. I know one guy who's been at the same desk in San Francisco since 1941. He was an ensign then and he's a lieutenant commander now, and all the bastard knows about salt water is that you cook potatoes in it."

Woodley said, "I know some guys who keep asking for overseas duty."

"Yes," said Dutton, "you hear that stuff but you never see it. I want to meet the guy who asks for sea duty."

"I've met some," Woodley said.

"So have I," I said. "Edwards has been putting in for sea duty every month. They keep telling him when his tour of duty here is up, they'll consider his request."

"Edwards is nuts," Dutton said. "Any guy who asks for trouble like that is a damn fool."

"I don't think so," Woodley said. "I'm going to ask for duty in the combat zone on my next assignment. I don't want somebody else doing my fighting for me."

"Go ahead," Dutton said. "Ask for action. Hell, ask for underwater demolition if you really want excitement. As far as I'm concerned, when my eighteen months are up, I'm going to ship over. I'll get thirty days' leave and then I'll come back here and sit the war out. It's dull but it's safe."

When the chaplain brought drinks to the table, Dutton asked him what he thought of requesting combat duty. The chaplain was a polite, nervous man.

"I don't know," he said. "That's something you've got to decide for yourself. I have bigger things to worry about."

"What's wrong, padre?"

"It's that loud speaker at the theater. Something always goes wrong with it during the sermon. When I first came here, services were held in the chapel. But I've built up such an interest that the chapel is too small. You many not know it but we had eighty-six men attend last Sunday, and eighty-eight the Sunday before that. We use the theater now, but my voice simply will not carry back to the officers' section. That loudspeaker is indispensable. But something always goes wrong with it."

"Why don't you have Chief Walters fix it? He's in charge of maintenance."

The chaplain frowned. "Chief Walters isn't very reliable. I asked him to have the programs for the Easter service printed but he didn't get enough of them made. Some of the men didn't get the opportunity to mail them home. Souvenir programs, you know, with the names of the commanding officer and the chaplain on them. Very attractive."

"That's too bad," Dutton said. "Good publicity, that sort of thing."

"Well, it never hurts," said the chaplain.

"Padre," Bates said, "maybe it never hurts, but this kowtowing can be overdone. We don't have to take anybody's guff."

"Well, yes, of course, in a way," murmured the chaplain.

"You know," Bates went on, "the thing that bothered me most in indoctrination school was losing my independence. I hated being pushed around and saluting every damn officer who walked by."

"I didn't like it either," Dutton said.

"I didn't just dislike it," Bates said, "I hated it."

"You're right, Bates," Krueger said. "Say, did you see the redhead in the USO show yesterday? She looks like hot stuff."

"I've seen her," Bates said. "She's hot stuff all right, and Captain Bard has been hanging around her ever since she hit the island. If you think you can beat his time, go ahead."

Krueger said, dreamily, "Boy, what I could do to that redhead."

Suddenly Bates stood up, hissing, "Get up, you guys." The admiral was approaching our table. We rose and stood at attention.

"Good evening, gentlemen," he said.

"Good evening, sir," we murmured.

"You're helping Commander Pierce celebrate, I see."

"Yes, sir," said Bates. "Thank you, sir."

The admiral said something about the weather and looked at us standing stiffly, listening to him intently. Dutton was bending forward, mouth slightly open, smiling fatuously. Bates was nodding, his head bobbing vigorously after every remark the admiral made.

Soon after the admiral left, the party broke up. The steward said it was the most expensive party ever given on Adak.

Chapter 10

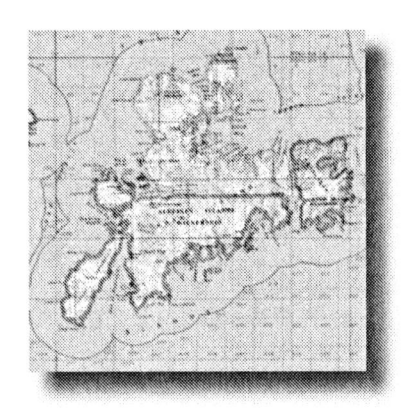

After Commander Pierce's plane left, about an hour before sunset on the Monday after his party, we drove back to our barracks.

"Well," Woodley said, "it looks as if I'm going to have to ask Dutton for Manley's furlough. I'd been hoping Pierce would leave you in charge of the office."

"Dutton made lieutenant one month before I did," I said. "You can't buck an AlNav. Dutton is my senior officer."

"I know, I know," Woodley grumbled, "but it would be a lot easier for Manley the other way."

"It certainly would. I'd be glad to recommend his emergency furlough. But I don't know whether Dutton will."

Woodley frowned. "Dutton's a peculiar guy. He is so damned cautious that it's almost a phobia with him. The other day Warren asked him to sign a chit for a light bulb that had burned out, but Dutton wouldn't do it. He said he didn't feel he had the specific authority to do it. Warren had to do without a light for two days, until Pierce got back from Kodiak.

I nodded. "He refused to OK Nooters' chit for a pair of shoes at the same time. He admitted that the shoes were worn out and had to be replaced, but he couldn't authorize it. I asked him later why he was so careful, and he told me he had learned the hard way. It seems that on his first assignment in the States he once signed something for an enlisted man and then got bawled out for it. Since then, he told me, he won't sign a thing if he doesn't have written authorization for it."

"Well, this is different," Woodley said. "Manley's cracking up. You don't go by the book when a man's life is concerned. I'll have to convince Dutton to make an exception this time."

But Woodley didn't get a chance to talk to Dutton until much later in the evening, for when we got back we found a crab-eating party going on. The previous evening Bates, the security office, and King, the boarding officer, had taken a small, converted yacht to the bay west of the island, dropped nets, and slept on the ship. In the morning they pulled up the nets and brought back dozens of giant crabs, some measuring almost three feet across. The men had boiled the crabs, broken off the enormous claws, and thrown away the small round bodies. Now they were sitting on the floor, cracking the claws open with hammers and pulling out the delicious white meat. Woodley and I joined them.

While we ate we listened to Bates discoursing on his favorite subject. Bates was fascinated by the notion of installing a brothel ship near the island. He was a large, gruff, loud man, and he had developed a method of talking that made many of his listeners laugh. It consisted of skillfully blending seemingly naive exaggeration with colossal profanity. He sometimes used pithier and shorter words than "goddamn," but ordinarily five or six common adjectives served his purposes. When he talked about the brothel ship, however, his voice softened and he looked longingly into space. "Think of it, boys," he would say. "There's a fortune in it, a goddamn fortune."

Bates mixed himself a drink, stretched out his feet on another chair, and said, "Boys, I'm a lawyer and I tell you legally there isn't a damn thing they could do to you. If you're three miles off shore, you're beyond the government's jurisdiction. Who's going to interfere?"

Bates looked around belligerently, but no one in the room had any intention of interfering. We had been through this discussion before; Bates's enthusiasm always revitalized it.

"How would you do it?' King asked.

"I'd get an LST that's been surveyed, one that's been through some damn invasion and isn't fit for service any more. I get it cheap, see, in San Francisco or Seattle. I hire twenty girls and put them aboard at Seattle. Once they're out on the ocean there isn't a damn thing they can do if they don't like it. Not a goddamn place to go. Where would they go?"

Bates paused but no one offered any suggestions. "See what I mean? I have a tug pull that LST up along the coast, through the Inland Passage, then along the chain to a spot three and half miles south of Adak. Right here, see?"

Bates stood up and pointed to a heavy dot on the large map on the wall. The spot had been clearly marked in previous sessions.

"How much would you charge?" King asked.

Bates put his drink down. "I've figured that pretty close. Twenty-five bucks is just about right. That includes the boat trip to the ship, one shot of whiskey aboard, fifteen minutes with a girl, and the trip back. Now anybody say that's too goddamned much?"

Nobody said it was too much. Bates continued, "There's ten thousand men on this island. And how many women? Say twenty nurses, right? Some of those girls are shacking up but it's private stock. No professionals. There's no natives on this goddamned island. Even the Aleuts had too much sense to stay here. Ten thousand men and no whores. I don't think twenty-five bucks is too much."

Bates paused, then looked at Dutton.

"Hell, I'm throwing in a free drink, see? You know what they're paying for whiskey now?"

Dutton said he didn't know.

"Forty bucks a fifth," said Bates, "when they can get it. They used to buy it from merchant ships, but the captain made me put marine guards on the dock. How can those poor bastards get their liquor?"

He looked at Dutton, and Dutton hurriedly admitted that he didn't know how the poor bastards could get their liquor.

"Yeh," Bates said, "you don't know. But I know, because I'm security officer. I know what's going on. They've got a still on a mountain, near the north end of the island. Poor bastards. Torpedo juice. Draining the alcohol out of the goddamned torpedoes. Ain't that a hell of a thing?"

Dutton said it was a hell of a thing.

"They can't get alcohol out of the hospital anymore," Bates explained. "The docs' got the stuff locked up. Even the corpsmen can't get it. So where's the seaman going to get it?" He shook his head sadly. "Torpedo juice. You know the guy who died last week? Food poisoning, they said. The hell it was. Torpedo juice. And some guys complain about twenty-five bucks, with a free drink."

"Nobody's complaining," King said. "What are you going to do about the braid?"

"Give them a pass," Bates said. "No use messing around with them. Passes to all admirals."

"How about the captains?" King asked.

"No," said Bates. "The hell with them. I'll give our captain a pass, and the exec. The rest of them can pay like anybody else."

The door opened and Edwards came in with the mail. King immediately opened his *Newsweek* to the pin-up and whistled. We looked appreciatively at the week's "near nude." King cut it out carefully, to hang in his room.

"Aren't you running out of wall space?" Woodley asked.

"No," King said. "I've got room for two more."

"What'll you do after that? Hang them on the ceiling?"

King considered the matter. "I don't think so," he said. "I'll probably take down the Sears and Roebuck ads. Come on in and I'll show you."

The walls in King's room were papered with pictures of girls. There were nudes, faces, and professional pornographic photos. On the wall alongside his bed, at the eye level of a man lying down, hung a series of enlarged photographs of an attractive woman. "I've been going with that gal a couple of years," King said. "We'll get married after the war. Ain't she pretty?"

He pointed proudly to the pictures by his bed. There were six of them. In the first, a dark-haired woman was smiling pleasantly. She was still smiling pleasantly in the next picture, but she had shed her coat in the interval. In succeeding pictures, the dress, slip, brassier, and pants, respectively, had been removed, so that the final photograph revealed a startlingly well-developed woman, still smiling.

"Ain't she pretty?" King asked again, looking thoughtfully at the picture of the woman he planned to marry.

We agreed that she was.

King had been a warrant officer in the regular navy for many years. When the war began he was commissioned a lieutenant (j. g.), but he apparently never felt that the commission was permanent. He spent a good deal of his spare time shining shoes. In the Aleutians we wore high, cumbersome, army boots. No one polished them except King. It was a labor of love with him. We sat around in the wardroom after dinner, talking or playing cribbage. King spread out newspapers in front of his chair and put out brown polish, rags, daubers, brushes, and water. Then for about an hour he worked on his shoes, scraping off the mud, wiping off the dust, cleaning, polishing, and shining.

When anyone teased him about it, he replied amiably that he didn't have much to do anyway. We could say what we liked, King told us, but Admiral Riley had once advised him that clean shoes were the mark of a gentleman. King had served, years before, on Admiral Riley's staff and relayed to us a number of the admiral's philosophical observations. The admiral regarded the Republican Party as dangerously radical, admired the poetry of Edgar Guest, and approved of old whiskey and young women.

King sometimes wrote letters to Admiral Riley, who was retired. King omitted the "j. g." in his own title and the "Ret." in the admiral's, and left the envelope lying around on his desk for days before mailing it.

In the morning King stepped out into the Aleutian mud and snow, and by the time he reached the dining room a hundred yards away, his shoes were as dirty as everyone else's.

King did not share the casual disregard for discipline that some reserve officers showed. He winced when Bates repeated the popular belief that rank among reserves is like virtue among whores. "You guys can talk," King said. "When the war is over you'll be civilians again. But not me. I got nine years to go before I retire."

It was not so much fear of getting into trouble as pure conditioning that made King behave so correctly. He was incapable of entering a room before a senior officer. A group of men would come to a door and start to walk in. King would stand aside until all senior officers and lieutenants had entered, then push back the j. g.'s and go in. Inasmuch as he was the boarding officer, this insistence on protocol sometimes proved embarrassing. King gathered in his boat the captains of several ships and brought them to the ship of the convoy commander. Then he sent them aboard in the order of rank. Being a j. g., he was always the last man to climb aboard and found the captains standing around awkwardly, waiting for someone to introduce them to the commander. Pierce urged King to disregard precedence and he once promised to do so. But he found it impossible.

"I'm sorry," he told us later. "I tried, but I couldn't. I started to climb the ladder and the I looked at those two lieutenant commanders waiting below me and I just couldn't do it."

It was generally felt that King's claim of friendship with Admiral Riley was largely imaginary, until the incident of the open scuppers. King had been complaining for some time about the captain of the *Saskatchewan,* an old Alaskan mariner who resented the navy's interference with a job he had been doing for twenty years. Once a rung on the *Saskatchewan* ladder broke while King was climbing aboard, and his boat fished him out of the water while the ship's crew jeered. Another time, the *Saskatchewan's* scuppers were opened at the precise moment that King was climbing down the ladder, and the toilet refuse drenched him. King swore that if that happened again he would write to Admiral Riley.

The next time the *Saskatchewan* was in port, its scuppers again were opened when King was on the ladder. He clambered into his boat, cursed out the jubilant crew and captain in language obscene and original, and sped to the shower. He came into the office sputtering, took out stationery, and wrote rapidly. He paused only once, to ask me, "Jack, if you had your choice of duty where would you rather go—Hawaii or California?"

"California," I said.

"Thanks," he said. He finished writing and addressed the envelope to Admiral Riley. This time he mailed the letter immediately.

Bates teased him about it that night while King, humming softly, polished his shoes. Two weeks later he came into the port office and said, "I think you better train somebody to take my place. I just got my orders."

"Where are you going?" I asked.

"California," he said. "Didn't I tell you I wrote the admiral?"

But this came later. We left King pinning the newly arrived picture on his wall and went back to the wardroom. "Where is Dutton?" Woodley asked.

"Gone to his room," Bates grunted. He was standing by the map, looking at a heavy dot just south of Adak.

"Do you want to come with me?" Woodley asked me.

"I don't think it'll help any," I said.

Woodley hesitated. "Maybe you better come along. I may need some help in persuading him."

Dutton greeted us politely, gave us the two chairs, and sat on the bed. As a fellow lodger, Dutton was certainly unobjectionable. He was quiet and reticent and spent much time writing to his wife and son, and he had a large picture of them on his dresser in his bedroom. It was the only picture in the room. On days when there was no mail he was likely to be depressed. He was especially edgy on days like this one, when the mail plane arrived without letters for him.

"The mail service is all fouled up," he said gloomily.

"It piles up once in a while," Woodley said. "Sometimes I get a bunch of letters at one time that had been written a week apart."

"I guess that's it," he said, relaxing a little. "I get worried when I don't hear from my wife. Have I ever shown you her picture?"

He had shown it to us many times but we looked again and Woodley said that she was a fine-looking woman. "What do you think of the boy?" Dutton asked.

Woodley and I said the appropriate things about the boy. Dutton smiled. "I was remembering today the first time I took the boy fishing. He was so excited he couldn't talk. All he could do was beam. When he caught his first fish he just hugged me. I wish you could have seen the look on his face. I'll never forget it. You know, it's a wonderful thing to trust someone completely. That boy trusts me."

Dutton was quiet for a while. He opened his wallet again, put the picture back, and said, "Security is the most important thing in the world."

I murmured something noncommittal. He went on. "This war interferes with all my plans. I've been paying on a retirement annuity that will start taking care of me when I'm fifty-five. I had it all figured out, but if this damn war lasts another year I'm going to fall behind on my payments."

He told me before that he had been the senior accountant in a large office. It was the highest job he could expect to hold with the firm, and he planned to keep it for eighteen more years and then retire. His annuity was expensive and he had been drawing on savings to pay it while he was in the service. But he couldn't afford to do that much longer.

"It's terrible that a man can plan his whole future, get it all protected, and then have everything upset by this lousy war," he said.

"All our lives have been upset," Woodley said.

"Woodley," he said, "I don't care about other lives. All I'm concerned with is my own. I have a wife and a son; I love them; and I don't give a damn about anything except getting back to them."

"If we lose the war," Woodley said, "life won't be very pleasant even with our families."

"If you really believe that," Dutton said, "you're a fool. I don't give a damn who runs the country—Democrats, Republicans, communists, or fascists. They're all out for themselves, and I'm out for myself. All I want is to be with my own family. I'll get along."

"The fascists and the communists may not let you get along."

"No," Dutton said, "you're wrong. The big changes won't come in my time. All I want to do is stall off trouble until I can retire. Then I don't care who runs the country. As long as they leave me alone they can do what they want."

Woodley said that the kind of society his son would have to live in might make a difference to the boy.

"That's his look-out," Dutton said. "I love the kid but I can't live his life for him. I've been on my own since I was sixteen. I'm building security for myself and by God I'm going to get it. I've got to stall them off until I retire."

"Well," said Woodley, "in a way, security is what we've come to talk to you about. Manley's security."

Dutton frowned but didn't say anything. We waited for a long time.

"Look," Woodley finally said, "all you have to do is approve an emergency furlough for Manley. Warren is willing to do Manley's work until he comes back. Or you can have a yeoman from the central office fill in for him. It can't do you any harm."

"Yes it can," Dutton snapped. "Pierce could give me hell for letting his yeoman go. No, sir."

"If he gets an emergency furlough, he'll be back before Pierce is. What have you got to lose?"

"I'm not sticking my neck out for Manley or you or anybody else."

Woodley looked angry for a moment, then bit his lip. "Manley isn't much good around the office any more," he said. "He just mopes around."

"I know," said Dutton. "I'm sorry. But I'm not taking any chances. Manley can wait another month."

"He can't. His wife is going out with another man."

Dutton smiled. "Hell, let her lay the guy for a month. Maybe she'll get tired of him and come back to Manley."

"Would you feel the same way about your wife?"

"That's one thing I don't have to worry about," Dutton said coldly. He stood up.

Woodley rose too. "The guy is close to cracking up. Doesn't that matter to you at all?"

"Yes," said Dutton. "I told you I'm sorry. But it matters more to me that I stay out of trouble. There isn't a thing you can do about it, so why not let it go at that? Good night."

We didn't bother to say good night.

Chapter 11

Woodley had hoped to see the captain on the following day but early in the morning the captain announced over the squawk box that an admiral was expected to fly in from the States during the day. The captain ordered all ships to get out into the bay and keep moving; he wanted the admiral to get the impression that everyone was busy at Adak and there was a great deal of activity going on. Dutton sent out both of the available patrol craft and all the minesweepers that were not in dry dock, and Woodley led all of his crash boats out to sea.

That evening when we went to the club, we saw several strange officers at the bar. They were the staff of the visiting admiral, and among them we suddenly recognized a familiar little round man.

Commander Wilson pumped our hands, patted our backs, and insisted on buying us drinks. We took a corner table and reminisced about indoctrination school.

"Three years," Woodley said, "and you're still in the navy."

Wilson lowered his voice. "I don't know, boys. Sometimes I think I should have taken that colonelcy."

"Don't you get along with the admiral?" I asked.

"The admiral is splendid. Very cooperative, very intelligent."

"How is the staff?" Woodley asked.

"Fine group of men. Friendly and helpful."

"What about your work?" I asked.

"Ah, my work. Don't let this get any farther, but the truth is I don't have anything to do."

"Aren't you the admiral's adviser on international law?"

"I am. When the admiral gets a problem involving international law I'm sure he'll ask my advice. We just haven't had any yet."

"But they must have given you something to do," Woodley said.

"Well, yes," said Wilson apologetically. "I serve on a number of boards."

"That sounds impressive. What boards?"

"Well, they're not really very impressive. I'm on the Ships Service Audit Board for one thing."

"What do you do?"

"At the end of each month I go through the ships service to check whether all the items listed in the inventory are actually in the store. At first I was afraid I'd have to count all the toothbrushes and candy bars and prophylactics and everything else. But I learned to check here and there and let it go at that."

"You know," Woodley said, "the PX manager told me he sells hundreds of rubbers every month. There are practically no women on the island. What on earth do they do with them?"

"I heard they put them on rifle tips to keep them dry," I said.

"Ye-es," said Wilson. "Perhaps. Anyway, once a month we go through the motions of checking all the items in ships service. The next day the audit board meets and the chairman, a supply corps commander, explains the long sheets of paper filled with figures that we have to sign. He talks about costs, sales, extensions, surveys, and inventories. We nod politely and sign dozens of papers. According to navy regs we are personally responsible for everything we sign, and I sometimes wonder about the quarter-million-dollar expenditures that I certify on those documents. But you could get neurotic if you took that sort of thing seriously."

"What else do you do?" Woodley asked.

Wilson smiled. "This will amuse you. I'm on the Seamanship Examination Board."

"No," I said, remembering Wilson's abysmal inability to understand anything in the seamanship class at indoctrination school.

"Yes, I'm chairman of the board that examines candidates for boatswain's mate. The other men on the board are a lieutenant, who was a lawyer, and a chief warrant, who has been in the navy thirty years. In the examinations we tend to let the warrant ask the questions. I sit by, trying to look wise. I've had a lot of practice trying to look wise."

"Don't you ever ask them anything?" I said.

Wilson looked at me sadly. "What could I ask them?"

I thought about it and decided that he was right. Woodley asked how long he expected to stay on Adak.

"Until tomorrow evening," Wilson said. "That will give us thirty hours here."

"Thirty hours is about right for duty in the Aleutians," Woodley said. "That's all anybody should be forced to spend here. I think I'll write to SecNav about it."

"Do that," Wilson said. "Be sure to send it through the chain of command."

"I'll send it in code," Woodley said. "I want SecNav to spend all day Sunday decoding my notion of Aleutian duty."

Wilson looked puzzled and Woodley told him about SecNav's Christmas message.

"The communications here are still sore about it. A couple of them in our barracks had to work overtime Christmas eve decoding the message. The Secretary of the Navy wanted to cheer us up. Now an ordinary guy might just say Merry Christmas and let it go at that. But not old SecNav. Four hundred groups in his message. And some dumb bastard in Washington encoded the message. Why would you encode a Christmas greeting? What's secret about it? It was the middle of the night in the Atlantic and they dragged communicators out of their sacks to break the message. They sure had a merry Christmas."

"I remember now," Wilson said. "Somebody in Washington finally spotted it, and they sent it in plain language the next day."

We talked about the foul-up and Wilson ordered more drinks and said, "You know, I'm surprised at how busy you people are here. As our plane approached the island today, I saw dozens of ships maneuvering all around the island."

Woodley laughed. "The truth is we have practically nothing to do. But the captain wanted your admiral to think we're busy, so the patrol craft doubled the patrols; my crash boats played tag; and the minesweepers were fishing. It must have looked impressive."

"It did to me," said Wilson, "but I'm afraid the admiral didn't see any of it."

"Why not?"

"He was asleep," Wilson said. "We didn't wake him until we were landing."

When we had finished drinking we took Wilson to our barracks. He stretched out comfortably in the lounge chair and took off his dusty shoes, at which King looked with disapproval. When we told King that Wilson was an old friend, King added Wilson's shoes to the pile of his own that he had spread out on a paper. King kept polishing shoes as we talked.

"The weather was perfect today," Wilson said. "We'd been hearing about the terrible Aleutian weather, but we certainly couldn't complain today."

"You were lucky," Woodley said. "This was one of the few good days. Usually we have a fog hanging over the island, sometimes low, sometimes high, in summer most of the time. That fog comes in awfully fast sometimes."

"It certainly does," I said, and told Wilson about the plane crash that Woodley had just been in. Wilson was very concerned, and Woodley had to reassure him that he hadn't been hurt.

"What's this williwaw I've been hearing about?" Wilson asked.

"Oh," Woodley said, "that's a winter wind. It comes in off the Artic, sometimes blows for a couple of days at a time, at its worst gets up to 100-mile gusts. We've had forty-foot waves in these waters.

"It's hard to describe the winter here to someone who hasn't been through it. Last New Year's day, when we awoke in the morning, it was pitch black and there was a continuous dull roar outside, like heavy static. Going from the barracks to the mess hall—a couple of hundred yards—took almost ten minutes. We wrapped ourselves up tight in parkas, with the hoods pulled down over our heads and only the tips of our noses showing. We walked at about a 60-degree angle, with the wind holding us up and pushing us back, and we called out a few words to each other but we couldn't hear anything. In the mess hall the walls—excuse me, Wilson, you call them bulkheads, I'm sure—shook, wobbled, and swayed. A wall in one of the Quonset huts collapsed in the middle of the night over a sleeping man, forming a kind of tent around him. He woke up, said, 'I'll be damned,' and went back to sleep. A jeep that had been left too near a crevice was blown over the side. They told me later it was a 70-mile wind, with gusts to 90. It blew like that for 36 hours."

King finished shining the shoes and gave Wilson a highly polished pair. Woodley looked at them and laughed. "Remember all the demerits you got for not keeping your shoes shined in indoctrination school?"

Wilson smiled wryly. "I've been trying to forget," he said. "But tell me, Jack, where did you go after indoctrination school?"

"I went to communications school. It's a long story, and Woodley's heard it before."

"Tell it again, Jack," Woodley said. "I'll make sandwiches for us." He took bread and ham out of the large refrigerator in the wardroom, made the sandwiches, and passed them out.

"Well," I said, "Woodley enjoyed his training at small boat school, but I'm afraid I didn't like everything that happened at communications school. The first night, tired of moving and registering, I went to bed at ten. A half-hour later, just as I was falling asleep, a harsh jangling bell rang loudly in our hallway. I jumped out of bed. My roommates explained that this was the preparatory bell, reminding us that it was time to go to bed. I crawled back into my upper bunk and had fallen asleep when a tremendous racket broke out. Bells rang, buzzers shrilled, chimes sounded. Again I jumped out of bed, to learn that this was the eleven o'clock 'tattoo.' When the clatter subsided, the loudspeaker blared taps from a phonograph record. It took me a long time to go to sleep that night.

"We spent a good deal of time preparing for a parade that was never held. In his welcoming address the captain told us that there was a critical shortage of trained communicators and that the school was going to utilize every minute to prepare us for our jobs. But shortly after that a parade was scheduled, and for a month we spent an hour a day drilling.

"Our part in the parade was simple. We were to march from the school to the stadium, then turn left and march past the reviewing stand. After that we were to turn left again and march back to school. It was not a very complicated maneuver and we mastered it, with reasonable skill, by the end of the first hour. After two drills we were executing the march and turn as well as we would ever do it. But the parade was not due for another three and a half weeks, so we continued practicing every day, to the beat of an amplified metronome. Then it rained on parade day and the whole thing was called off.

"The communications school was stationed at one of the oldest universities in the country, and in our hall were listed the names of all the men who had once occupied those rooms. After five months in that ugly, drafty room on the fourth floor, I developed considerable sympathy for Henry David Thoreau and understood why he left the university a cantankerous critic, subject to tuberculosis, and eager to live alone in a shack by Walden Pond.

"On the second day I stopped to watch a quaint spectacle on the famous campus. In the middle of the quadrangle twelve officers stood in line. One of them marched forward three paces, looked straight ahead, and shouted, 'Company, attention!' he paused for a moment and I looked around to see whom he was addressing. There was no one. 'Right face,' he shouted, and I started to obey before I realized that he probably didn't mean me. 'Left face!' he roared. 'About face!' 'To the rear march!' 'Company halt!'

"He marched back into line smartly and the man next to him marched forward, drew a deep breath, and shouted the same commands. Two officers with notebooks in their hands were standing at one side, taking notes. I asked a man near me what was going on.

"'They're trying out for company officers,' he said. 'The one who shouts loudest is going to be company commander. The two next loudest will be in charge of sections. That second guy from the left will probably be a commander. You could hear him way out on the square.'

"I looked at two spectators, a man with a goatee, smiling wryly, and a distinguished-looking old man staring in dazed disbelief. The campus must have seemed strange to the faculty. That evening, when we lined up for retreat, the man who could be heard in the square was our new commander.

"It was fashionable to pretend we were working under terrific pressure, and a favorite remark in letters sent home was, 'I dropped my pencil in the radio class this morning and missed a month's work.' Actually, we could have left the pencil on the floor permanently for all the good that particular course did us. The university's civilian instructors, who were supposed to give us a quick course in radio theory, taught it. Since none of us had any mechanical training, we were totally confused from the start. Our teacher was a conscientious and intelligent Englishman who tried hard to make us understand radio. He didn't succeed.

"The instructors were responsible for getting us through the course. They could hardly admit their failure to teach us, so they graded generously. When I found my grade of 25 percent was worth a 'B,' I stopped worrying about the courses and sat back, listening to our instructor's pronunciation. He had a charming accent and considerable command of stylistic devices. I enjoyed his delivery immensely, although I had only a faint notion of what he was talking about. The instructor preferred my misplaced attention, I think, to the attitude of students who read newspapers in class.

"It was not this instructor but his successor, an older man, who told us as he returned our examination papers, 'Teaching is the imparting of the incomprehensible to the ignorant by the incompetent.' He seemed particularly dejected that day, although we gave him sufficient cause for dejection every day. Dr. Henning was a fat little man who had been pulled out of a research laboratory to teach us radio theory. He wore a little portable microphone around his neck, which made his timid voice audible in the large classroom. It also made embarrassingly audible his coughs, snorts, rumbles, and sniffles. And since he was an inarticulate individual, many awkward noises interrupted the hesitant progress of his lectures.

"On the board, when we came into his classroom, were the intricate components of a radio circuit, vari-colored lines, circles, squares, and formulas. Dr. Henning reminded us that he had explained in previous lectures how the vacuum tube worked. This time he would illustrate how it affected the radio circuit. He talked for a while, using terms like 'magnetic field' and 'grid' and 'volts.' The class stared at him blankly and he glanced desperately around the room, looking for a sign of understanding. When in the course of this futile search his eyes fell on me, I nodded vigorously. It seemed little enough to do for a man who was trying so hard. But it wasn't enough. A few minutes later Dr. Henning got confused again, waved his arms, pointed helplessly to the board, and murmured unconvincingly, 'I think you will agree that the current must be stepped up at the grid to get across.'

"One of my roommates was having almost as much difficulty with communications as you, Wilson, had had with indoctrination. Kendall was familiar enough with the university, having earned a Ph.D. in English there before the war, but he could not adjust to the new tempo. Something had been disturbed in the campus atmosphere, he said, and he wandered around vaguely trying to find out what it was. For most of us there were some new things to learn, but to Kendall everything was strange.

"At nine o'clock we had a class in Morse code and at ten we took typing. Some of the men knew the code and were learning to type. Some knew how to type and were learning code. But Kendall knew neither code nor typing. After two weeks we sat tensely over our typewriters, earphones on our heads, laboriously typing out the sound we heard. We tried to look like characters in melodramatic movies, receiving urgent messages, a pretense made somewhat difficult by the fact that what we usually received were word groups like PBJXU or sentences like 'I love my little dog.'

"We hunched over our typewriters and recorded what we heard. All of us, that is, except

Kendall. When he was under pressure, the only letter he could find was 'J.' His right forefinger responded adequately, but none of the others did. Kendall heard a dit-dot, thought for a moment, recognized it as 'A,' and began looking for 'A.' It was always hiding. While he searched, another sound came through his earphones. If he kept looking for the 'A' he didn't hear the new sound clearly. If he listened to the sound he didn't get the 'A' recorded. After a little while he dropped his hands disconsolately on his lap and just listened.

"Then Maud came over. The typing teachers, whom we called Maud and Gertrude, unintentionally inspired us. We felt that if those two prissy characters could be officers in the navy, we certainly could. Maud saw that Kendall wasn't typing and sidled over, counting aloud, 'One, two, *three*, four.' (Gertrude counted 'One, two, three, *four*,' and they had once had a public disagreement over the two methods.)

"'Why aren't you typing?' Maud asked.

"'I can't find the letters,' Kendall said.

"Maud looked at him suspiciously. 'Here are the letters,' he said.

"'I mean I can't find them in time to type the code,' Kendall explained. Maud would then put him to work copying from the practice book for the rest of the hour. The next day Kendall would sit down with his earphones and type a letter, or two letters if 'J' happened to be the first one, and then put his hands in his lap again.

"After one of these unproductive sessions Kendall walked out of class with me. 'I think I'll see the captain,' he said. 'I'll tell him I want to drop a few courses. My schedule is too heavy.'

"I tried to be tactful. 'This isn't graduate school,' I pointed out. 'You can't drop courses in the navy.'

"'I'll explain it to him,' said Kendall. He came from Vermont and was inclined to be stubborn.

"At the end of the month the personnel officer sent for him. When Kendall came back he seemed stunned. 'I have orders to report in San Francisco Saturday,' he said.

"'What kind of duty?' I asked.

"'Do you remember when I went to see the captain? He asked me whether I preferred amphibious duty or small craft. I chose amphibious.'

"'Amphibious isn't bad,' someone said dubiously.

"'I don't know,' Kendall said, 'and it doesn't look as if I'm going to find out. It's the armed guard school I have to report to.'

"After Kendall left, our squad executed its maneuvers a little more gracefully, but we never really attained military dignity. When we marched to classes we sang; sometimes we sang 'Anchors Aweigh,' although it was not one of our favorites. We preferred ditties like:

> The Waves and Wacs will win the war
> So what in hell are we marching for

and

> When the war is over we will all enlist again
> We will like hell we will

"For a few days all the squads bellowed a somewhat irrelevant song as we marched down the campus. A former boy scout had dug it up from recollections of childhood, and it went like this:

> Be kind to your web-footed friends
> A duck may be somebody's mother
> Be kind to our friends of the swamp . . .

"We did not know the fourth line and always broke off abruptly after 'swamp.' The captain heard us singing it one day and looked at us thoughtfully. On the bulletin board the following morning we found a list of songs naval officers were permitted to sing while marching. There was no duck song on the list.

"In making up coded messages we were warned against using slang. It seemed that early in the war a Wave, breaking messages in Washington, suddenly fainted. An indelicate communicator in the North Atlantic had radioed, 'Send more blankets. It's cold as a witch's tit.'

"We were also advised that dispatches should be sent only when necessary, and that a ship at sea should never break radio silence except in emergencies. Our instructor told us of a captain who enjoyed making up clever phrases for 'padding' his messages. Every time he thought one up, he ordered his communicator to send out a dispatch using his witticism. He was shortly given a change of duty, the instructor said.

"In the class on procedures at sea we would pretend that the instructor's platform was the bridge of a war vessel. Lieutenant Lovett, the instructor, would give commands; men would hoist flags and say 'Aye aye, sir,' heartily; and on the whole the technique was interesting and educationally sound. But it lost some of its effectiveness after the incident with Ensign Bradley.

"Bradley was a naive young fellow who had been sent from college straight into communications school. He was earnest and hardworking, but he tended to get excited in new situations. Lieutenant Lovett called him up to the platform.

"'We're going to see how you handle this problem, Bradley,' he said. 'Stand up here on the bridge.'

"'Yes, sir,' said Bradley, leaning on the lecturer's rostrum.

"'You're the officer of the deck. The captain is asleep and when this problem comes up you won't have time to call him. You'll have to give orders yourself.'

"'Aye aye, sir,' said Bradley.

"'All right, here it is. You see a torpedo heading for your ship from the port side at a forty-degree angle. It is three hundred yards distant. What orders will you give?'

"'Just a minute,' sputtered Bradley. 'What's the angle?'

"'Forty degrees. And now it's only two hundred yard distant.'

"'Oh my God,' wailed Bradley. 'What side is it coming from?'

"'Port side. It's a hundred yards away. What do you say?'

"'Abandon ship,' yelled Bradley. 'Abandon ship right now!'

"The school prepared us for the chain of command that we would find in the navy by establishing a pattern of responsibilities. The pattern began in the room we lived in. One of us had to act as senior officer of room 410 and another as assistant senior officer. Since there were only three of us, the titles did not really impress us. Each squad had a leader, an assistant leader, and a roll-call taker. Every two squads had a section leader as well as an assistant section leader. And at the top of the pyramid was our company commander, Lieutenant Rush.

"Rush was a short man with a tremendous voice who walked briskly, articulated carefully, and saluted frequently. He took his position very seriously and was often out in his place a good ten minutes before assembly time. He implored us to beat Company C into formation. Companies A and B were three and two months, respectively, senior to us, and apparently Rush had given up hope of our surpassing them. But he watched Company C with jealous hatred and repeatedly insisted that we could be a hell of a lot better company than they were, if we would only get the lead out and run to formations. 'I tell you guys,' he would plead, 'that Company C isn't worth a damn. We can look better and march better than them any day of the week. So for Christ's sake, you guys, get on the ball.'

"He was very earnest, and some of us may have felt badly about not being on the ball and resolved to make Company D a better company. I don't remember that I did.

"Company Commander Rush spent a good deal of time, when he was not urging us to hurry, looking up at the sky. When the weather looked threatening, Rush spent almost all his time looking up. He was responsible for change of uniform: we were forbidden to change clothes until officially ordered to do so. When it looked like rain, Rush would announce over the loudspeaker system that boomed through the college yard, 'Now hear this. The uniform of the day is gray, with raincoats.' We would run to the dormitories and get our raincoats. After the rain stopped, Rush would announce, 'Now hear this. The uniform of the day is gray.' We would take off our raincoats.

"The system did not always work perfectly. One day we were about to march off to class when Rush was called to the captain's office. The assistant company commander ordered us to march to class. At that moment it began to rain. The assistant felt that he was substituting for Rush-the-company-commander, not Rush-the-uniform-changer. He refused to assume any extra responsibilities, and we marched six blocks in a downpour, past the dormitories in which our raincoats were hanging. On another occasion Rush told us to put on raincoats, then went away for the day. It never did rain, but we marched the rest of that hot and humid day in our coats.

"One of my roommates, Ed Willis, kept worrying about what expression to assume while standing at attention. We had fewer formations in communications school than there had been in indoctrination school, and the subject didn't particularly interest me. But Ed was a pleasant chap, and to humor him we discussed it for a few minutes before turning to the main activity of the evening, which was usually poker.

"'I was talking to a guy in Company B today,' Ed said. 'He says a guy ought to have a blank look on his face when he is being inspected.'

"Bill Lawson, who was really interested only in girls, said, 'We used to look determined at indoctrination school. Somebody told me they like you to look real earnest, like you were going to fight the next minute.'

"'I don't know,' Ed said. 'I tried to look determined last Saturday. The captain stared at me and said, "What are you frowning at? Don't you like it here?"'

"'I told him I liked it fine. He glared for a while and said, "Your uniform isn't pressed. Why don't you put on a clean one for inspection?"'

"'This is a clean one,' I told him, and he barked, "Where do you keep it? In a shoe box?"'

"'One of the inspecting officers burst out laughing and the captain relaxed. He pretended he was still mad, but he didn't tell the yeoman to write anything down. Then the photographer came along and the captain forgot all about me.'

"Every month a class book was compiled for the new graduates, so the photographers were busy on Saturday morning recording the weekly inspection. The captain was a vain man but not a subtle one. He would strut down the inspection line, always facing the camera. Often he paused, hand extended in executive gesture, until the photographers, who were supposedly taking candid shots, had time to get the right angle and snap him. The captain inspected only the front row. He sent the executive officer to examine the back lines, which didn't show up in the pictures.

"The duller phases of a trainee's life didn't show up in the photos, either. On the morning watch, having guarded a cold hallway in Massachusetts since four o'clock, I decided that there has been too much sentimental nonsense written about the beauty of the sunrise. It may be that you need the proper setting for that sort of thing, but the sunrise rarely seemed to me sufficient case for jubilation. It was hard to believe that it was a genuinely important element in the nation's security.

"The school demanded correct naval terminology, and when the watch officer in the next hallway relieved me for breakfast, I wrote carefully in the log: "0600. Shoved off for chow." This may have been overdoing it, for all I did was cross the courtyard to eat breakfast, but the regulations required it.

"We were supposed to record in the log the arrival of anyone after hours. This sometimes created a dilemma. We didn't want to report our fellow students, yet anyone caught failing to report a late arrival was subject to severe penalty. We found ways of solving the problem. One night at 0100 a man came down to invite me to a poker game on the third floor.

"'I'd like to but I can't,' I said. 'I'm on watch here.'

"'Why don't you come up and have a look,' he urged. 'It's a good game.' He kept looking at the open entrance door nervously.

"'All right,' I said. 'I'll take a look at the game.'

"We walked slowly up the stairs. The poker players held up the game to greet me. They were friendly men and extremely interested in me. I had to tell them where I came from and what I did and what I thought of things in general. I never had a more appreciative audience. Finally another man slipped into the room and nodded unobtrusively to the man who had brought me up.

"'It's been good to know you,' said my host. 'I guess the boys are going to break up for the night now.'

"I said goodnight and walked slowly down the stairs. The entrance door was closed now. When the clock struck again I wrote in the log: '0200. All secure.' I wrote it neatly and plainly and then took out a detective story and read for an hour. Then I took time out to write '0300. All secure,' before going back to my book.

"One Saturday night, about a month before we graduated, our company was permitted to have a stag party in a large hall near the campus. The men drank a lot of beer; they booed all of the acts except the strip teaser, whom they forced to dance in the nude for a half hour; they broke a few windows on the way home. The same night a block away from the stag, three middle-aged-couples were arrested. They were playing penny poker, at one minute past midnight, in the home of one of the couples.

"By now we felt that we had accumulated considerable knowledge at the communications school. We had learned that it was dangerous to address a warrant officer as 'chief.' We knew that the standard variation on 'sighted sub, sank same,' was 'Sighted sub, glub, glub.' We liked to use the expression, 'I was volunteered for it.' And, unlike ordinary mortals, we could now communicate by blinking lights, pressing buzzers, waving flags with both arms, and hoisting flags in specific arrangements. But I still thought that our illustrious predecessor at the university, Henry David Thoreau, was right when he suggested that neither lights nor sounds nor semaphores nor flags were especially helpful to a man who didn't have anything important to communicate.

"Until the last two weeks of our training we had been taught largely what to do *on* the water. Now we were given a series of lectures on what to do *in* it. The officer who gave us this advice had spent his entire naval career at the communications school, and his first tip to us was a memorable one. 'If you find yourself in the drink in the Pacific,' he said, 'swim east or west. There is more chance of finding land than if you swim north or south.' He liked to use phrases like 'in the drink,' and he told us that the shark has very poor vision. The barracuda is a coward and can sometimes be frightened by splashing. The sting of the Dutch jellyfish hurts, but if one grits one's teeth the pain eventually goes away. The best food with which to jump overboard, our lecturer said, is a head lettuce. It has high water content. I tried to visualize myself jumping overboard with a head lettuce under one arm.

"About this time, too, we were asked about our preference in locale for the next tour of duty. Ed Willis and I filled out the form perfunctorily, sharing the general suspicion that the navy used the information only to determine where not to send people. But my other roommate, Bill Lawson, came in that evening humming happily. He brought a large box that he proudly opened for our inspection. It was full of beads, colored glass, dime bracelets, and whistles.

"'That's for the girls,' Bill said, winking lewdly.

"'What girls?' Ed asked.

"'The native girls,' Bill explained. 'I've asked for duty in the South Pacific.'

"He looked at the box of trinkets affectionately. 'I hope the war doesn't last more than three years,' he said. 'I figure I have enough here to last that long.'

"The strange thing is that Bill *was* assigned to the South Pacific. And that was just about three years ago."

It was late, so I took Wilson back to the club.

Chapter 12

When Dutton stepped out of the office the following morning, Manley went over to Woodley's desk. He had always been thin but I was suddenly startled by how gaunt he looked. His eyes were dull behind the brass-rimmed glasses and his voice was dull.

"Did you find out anything, Mr. Woodley?" he asked.

"I'm having dinner with the captain tonight. I promise that I'll ask him about helping you."

Manley turned away and slouched back to his chair. "That's my last chance," he muttered. "If the captain says no, there's only one thing I can do."

Woodley and I exchanged quick glances. If Manley didn't get help soon, it would be too late to help him at all. But the chance was there, because the captain liked Woodley. He liked him not because Woodley was a good officer but because Woodley was an excellent baseball player. The captain was crazy about baseball. During the spring he had quietly signed up players for his team, then announced that there would be a summer tournament. The other teams had to pick their players from the remaining men.

The captain took his baseball seriously. That summer, while marines were invading Pacific islands and fleets were converging on Japan, he carried out his naval duties adequately but he moved dinnertime up a half-hour so that the game could start earlier. He was usually the first man on the field, wearing a baseball cap at a cocky angle, a busy, portly, short man playing first base. He didn't get many hits and he made occasional errors, but no one contested the first baseman's job with him.

I found playing second base something of a psychological hazard. Once, when a ground ball went through the captain, I called, "Nice try." He glared at me. Next time it happened I said, "I should have gotten it," and the captain nodded agreeably. In one of the early games I dropped a fly ball and heard the captain angrily muttering about unsatisfactory fitness reports. Since the fitness report is the most important part of a naval officer's record, I was disturbed. But an inning later I hit a triple and the captain patted me on the back and said I was a good man.

His favorite, though, was Woodley, who was the best pitcher in the league. We lost only one game all summer, and that was when Woodley was standing an O.O.D. watch. The captain was furious when he learned that Woodley was on duty and sent an officer to relieve him immediately. But by the time Woodley arrived we were losing by five runs and we never did catch up. It seemed to me that the captain's dislike for Commander Henry stemmed from the latter's lack of foresight on that occasion.

Even after the season ended, the captain sometimes called us on the squawk box. "Send in Lieutenant Woodley," he would order Dutton. Dutton would pass the word to Woodley and then would say to me, "I wonder why the captain keeps sending for him." Once I asked Woodley what the captain wanted. "Nothing much," he said. "Just wanted to talk baseball. Today we were going over the game with the Air Station."

"That's the one he got a double in, wasn't it?'

"That's the one."

So the captain was always pleasant to Peter Woodley, but Woodley had never taken advantage of the friendship until he arranged a dinner invitation so that he could intercede for Manley.

That evening I was watching in the wardroom, waiting for Woodley to come back from the captain's dinner, when Bates burst into the room. "Boys," he announced loudly, "you know what the captain did today? He put me in charge of the goddamned fire department. Ain't that a doozey? All I know about fire departments is that the damn trucks are red."

Bates was obviously in good humor. He mixed himself a Scotch-and-soda, took a couple of drinks, then put down his glass and extracted a newspaper clipping from his wallet. "Did I show you guys this?"

"What is it?" King asked.

Bates gave it to him. "Read it," he said. "Show it to the boys."

King held up the clipping, a feature story and a blurry picture of a navy officer. The caption on the picture was "Fighting Dan."

"Who is that?" I asked.

"Lieutenant Daniel Bates," King read aloud.

Bates grinned. "That's me."

"'Fighting Dan,'" said King. "Who did you ever fight?"

"All right," Bates said. "Cut the crap. Just read it."

King read aloud. "'Lieutenant Bates has been overseas with our gallant navy during the past year.' I'll be damned. 'Fighting Dan.' The only fight you've done is in line at the bar."

"That's all right," Bates said. "How about those guys who got stateside duty?"

"Listen to this," King said. "'Lieutenant Bates's splendid record culminated in his promotion last month.' Why, Bates, the only record you've made is perfect attendance at the movies."

"Oh yeah?" Bates growled.

"Congratulations," King said. "All the other guys were promoted because they were j. g.'s for fifteen months. I'm glad you made it on merit."

"Well," I added, "merit and fifteen months."

"The hell with you guys," Bates said. "Give it back to me."

"What paper is it from?" I asked.

"It's a local paper," Bates mumbled.

"What's the name of it?"

"Well," Bates said, "it's a specialized paper."

"Yeh," said King. "What's the name of it?"

"The Boilermakers' Journal."

"What are you doing in *The Boilermakers' Journal?"*

"My father's an official in the union," Bates said. "Any of you guys want another drink? I got another bottle here. And there's some canned chicken in the refrigerator."

Bates's reference to Scotch and chicken reminded me that in all the war stories I had read, complaints about the food were vehement. Our food had been good. We never had Spam or C rations or the other canned atrocities. The powdered milk did taste like chalk ground in vinegar, and the powdered eggs were mildly nauseating. But one could do without milk and eggs when meats and fish and vegetables were tastily prepared. There was fog, monotony, dullness, confinement, and isolation, but the navy food was good.

The army didn't eat as well, and its officers often found excuses to visit our dining room. Hordes of them showed up on steak nights, until our mess steward began posting misleading menus. In the morning announcements he sometimes listed steak as macaroni and sometimes as lamb stew. The army resented this duplicity, but food was the only compensation for the drabness of Aleutian life.

I watched Dutton playing cribbage with Leary, a communications officer. Leary had played cribbage every evening since he arrived on the island. Even on the night he gave the customary party to celebrate his promotion, he put out food and drinks for the guests and then organized a cribbage game. Only one subject ever drew him willingly away from the game: a discussion of getting back to the States sooner than expected. To him the casual remark, "How much longer you got to go?" was no casual remark. And when Dutton made the remark, as Leary was putting away the cribbage board for the evening, Leary replied earnestly, "Four months and twenty-one days."

Leary poured his nightly glass of powdered milk and said, "The boys at the comm office were talking today. One of them read an article that said a couple of American generals had been asked what the 'four freedoms' were, and they didn't know."

Dutton snorted. "Why should they?"

"That's what the boys were saying, what the hell difference did it make?"

We tested ourselves, and it turned out only one man knew them. He happened to remember them because he'd been assigned to pin up the 'four freedoms' posters.

"Why does it bother you?" Dutton asked.

Leary hesitated. "I don't know. It doesn't bother me. It just surprised me."

"What did the boys say?" I asked.

"They didn't care. It was just something to talk about. You know, you talk about women, and you bitch about the exec, and you listen to scuttlebutt about this and that. And this story about the 'four freedoms' came up, and everyone said it was a silly story. The guy who wrote the article was upset because the generals didn't know about the 'freedoms,' but nobody else in the service knows about them or takes them seriously. They couldn't see what the fuss was about."

"They're damn right," Bates said. "That better-world crap is all right for political speeches, but I never met anybody who believes it. Except crackpots. Well, we're not fighting for a better world, we're just trying to keep the one we've got from getting worse. And even for that you couldn't get enough men if you didn't have the draft. Hell, I don't expect the world to be any better after the war, and I sure don't want my personal world to be worse. But that's no reason for pretending there's a lot of silly ideals mixed up in it. How about that?"

"You're right," Dutton said. "I don't know whom the propaganda boys think they're kidding, but I'm like you. I've never met anybody who believed in that crap. As far as I'm concerned, everybody is out for himself, and the sooner we all admit it the better off we'll be. How many guys do you know who don't want stateside duty? And how many guys respect a uniform when a son-of-a-bitch like Henry is in it? I'll tell you what you want. It's the same thing

I want—to get back home just as soon as we can. And the minute the war ends you'll hear so much screaming to get out of uniform, you'll forget you ever heard this 'freedoms' baloney."

I had never seen Dutton get so wound up, and he noticed that I was watching him. "Getting pretty late," he said. "I'm going to bed."

Everyone except Bates and me went to bed.

"Ain't you sleepy?" Bates asked.

I told him that I was waiting to see Woodley and find out about Manley.

"Which guy is Manley?" Bates asked.

"He is our yeoman, quiet guy about thirty-five."

Bates remembered. "What's his trouble?"

I was telling him when Woodley came back.

"What did the captain say?" I asked him.

"I think he'll OK it—if he remembers. He was pretty high when I left him, and he was still drinking. I'll remind him tomorrow."

Bates shook his head. "What do you want to get mixed up with that for? You bother the captain and you get Dutton mad. What do you care about a goddamn yeoman?"

"Look," Woodley said. "The commander is on leave. The disbursing officer had ten days' leave to take care of private business. The doc just had a week in Seattle. But here is a guy whose marriage is breaking up, and he can't get away to try and save it."

"Hell," said Bates, "he's better off without her. If she's laying somebody now, she'll do it again."

"That's for Manley to decide," Woodley said. "This way he has no choice."

"OK," said Bates. "It's your funeral, not mine."

Chapter 13

After breakfast we drove to the Red Cross office. The fog hung below the mountaintops and wisps of it floated around the island. The bay was dull gray, the snow was dull gray, and the sky was dull gray.

Woodley told Saunders about his talk with the captain and asked what would be the best way of following it up. Saunders suggested that Woodley take Manley's leave request directly to the captain. We would be violating the chain of command, for Dutton was acting head of the department, but if the captain spoke to him Dutton wouldn't dare reject Manley's request.

When we came back to the port office, Dutton was arguing with the personnel officer.

Rivers was explaining that he was sending a new quartermaster to replace Warren, whose tour of Aleutian duty would end soon. The new quartermaster was named James Telford. He was, Rivers said, competent, courteous, and colored.

"I won't have him in my office," Dutton said. "I don't care how good he is."

"Look," Rivers said, "I've shown you the *Navy Bulletin* that says we are to treat Negroes the same as Whites. If it's the official navy policy, it ought to be safe enough even for you."

Rivers was referring to Dutton's persistent refusal to sign anything until he found official authority for so doing. He knew that Dutton signed absolutely nothing until he was shown in navy regs or an AlNav or an official *Navy Bulletin* that he had specific authority to take action. It took a long time to get ink for our office, or a parka for an enlisted man, or permission to leave the office five minutes early.

But this time even official authority was not enough to convince Dutton. "I don't care what it says," he told Rivers. "You can't make me take a nigger in this office and you know it."

"Listen," Rivers said. "Telford is the most qualified man for the job; he is a nice guy; and he is going to work here. I'm sending him over in a few minutes."

"You send him," Dutton said, "and when I get through with him he'll go back and tell you himself that he doesn't want to work here."

"Do you know him?" Rivers asked.

"I don't know him and I don't want to know him." Dutton flung open the manila folder on his desk and began to study it. Rivers walked out.

Woodley and I stepped out in the hall. We agreed that it would be foolish to talk to Dutton about Manley while he was so angry. Woodley went to the captain's office and I went back to my desk.

A few minutes later the squawk box buzzed and the captain's voice said, "Mr. Dutton."

Dutton pressed the buttons nervously, cleared his throat, and said cheerily, "Yes, sir."

"Dutton," the voice said, "I understand a yeoman in your office is having domestic trouble and wants an emergency leave."

"Yes, sir," Dutton said.

"I wonder whether we couldn't arrange to let him go."

"Of course, sir," Dutton said. "I'll be very happy to do it."

"Thank you," the captain said.

Dutton pressed the buttons back in place and looked at me. "You and Woodley put one over on me, eh?"

"No," I said, "we made it easy for you. Since it was the captain who suggested it, you aren't responsible, and the commander can't blame you."

Dutton glared at Manley, the muscles twitching in the corners of his mouth. "All right, yeoman," he said, "you get your leave."

Manley looked at him listlessly and said, "Yes, sir." He began to open drawers and take things out of them. Dutton watched him malevolently. Then he looked up; his eyes brightened; and he sat up straight. A slim, clean-cut young Negro stepped into the room. He was dressed neatly and his shoes sparkled. He looked around the office and stepped toward Dutton's desk.

"I'm Telford, sir," he said. "Lieutenant Rivers told me to report here for duty."

Dutton stared at him coldly, then said, "Do you want to work here?"

"Yes, sir."

"What's the matter, are you afraid of sea duty?"

"No, sir. I've had thirty-two months of sea duty. I had my appendix removed two weeks ago, and Lieutenant Rivers is giving me shore duty for a while."

Dutton looked at him for a long time, then, speaking slowly and pronouncing his words very distinctly, he said, "I want you to know that nobody in the world can make me treat you like a white man. Your race is inferior and it smells. I don't want any member of your race working in this office. Do you understand?"

Telford had been looking at him intently. He paled, and his hands trembled a little. He said, in a voice that tried to be restrained but was hoarse, "You cheap son-of-a-bitch. If we were out of uniform I'd knock your teeth out."

Dutton jumped out of his chair. "What's that?" he screamed. "I'll have you up for court martial. I've got witnesses here."

"The hell you have," Woodley said. He was standing in the doorway. "I didn't hear Telford say a word. Did you, Jack?"

"No," I said. "I haven't heard anything."

Woodley looked at Manley. "Not me," Manley said. "I didn't hear it."

Warren looked up. "No, sir," he said. "Haven't heard a thing."

Woodley looked at Dutton and smiled. Dutton was sputtering. Then the door to the ship-plot room opened and Nooters stepped in. Dutton pounced on him.

"Did you hear what this nigger called me?" he yelled.

Nooters looked at him impassively. "I didn't even know there was a colored man here," he said. He walked over to Telford and put out his hand. "I'm glad to know you," he said.

Telford shook his hand, looked at us and at Dutton, and walked out of the room. Woodley walked with him to the personnel office. Dutton turned to the window and looked out. I looked out the window too. The water was a dirty gray; the sky was a dirty gray; and the snow was dingy and splotched with black patches. The gray waves splashed against the docks with irritating monotony, and the buoys in the bay bobbed in the swell. The fog hung below the mountaintops, and wisps of clouds settled on high spots on the island.

Chapter 14

Woodley had mentioned a couple of times that Eva might get to Adak with her USO troupe. One evening he opened a pink letter and yelled out loud, "She's coming! She's coming! They'll be here next week."

Woodley was excited all week. He met the plane when it arrived, on the twentieth of July, and bounced happily into the post office a little later. "OK, boys, they're in. I've got a big date for tonight."

Even Commander Pierce was impressed. He had just returned from leave and was in good humor. "Who is it?"

"Eva Jensen, a girl I met just before I came out here. Her outfit is called Sweethearts on Parade, and they give their first show tonight. I'm going to pick her up after the show."

I offered Woodley my gray uniform, which was practically new. Pierce said that if Woodley wanted to use his Quonset that evening, he was welcome to it. Bates tried to push a package of prophylactics into Woodley's pocket.

Men kept dropping into the office and Woodley explained, repeatedly, that Eva was not that kind of a girl at all. Bates leered and said, "Sure, sure," and stuck around all afternoon.

At 1640 the army phoned the port office. One of their lookouts had seen four men in a boat who had landed on the southwest side of the island, looked around, then got back into the boat. He had shouted to them, but they had ignored him and sailed away. He couldn't identify the men in the sixty-foot motor launch.

The army wanted to know whether we had anyone in that vicinity. Dutton checked and announced that we hadn't. The area was dangerous; an incomplete survey had chartered some pinnacles and a few shallow spots. "They swept mines there a year ago," Dutton said, "but they worked only on clear days. I spent a week on a mine sweeper out there."

Pierce looked at the chart and said, "Dutton, you better go with Woodley in his crash boat. Try to find that damned boat before dark. The army says it may be Jap spies. I know better, but I've got to take action before I tell the captain about it. All right, you two, get going."

"Gee, commander," Woodley pleaded, "I got a date tonight."

"What time?"

"Eleven."

"Well," said Pierce, "you'll be back before then. Go on, get out there. I've got to report to the captain."

Woodley told me that if he wasn't back on time I should meet Eva at the theater and take her to the club to wait for him. Then he and Dutton hurried down to the dock, and a few minutes later the crash boat sped out of the bay.

We stayed by the port office radio during the dinner hour. At 1830 an army plane spotted the boat and gave its position. We radioed the information to Woodley's crash boat, just before the captain walked into the port office.

"Get me Bates on the phone," he told me. I located Bates and listened to the one-sided conversation.

"Bates," said the captain, "do the Japs have any sixty-foot motor launches exactly like ours?"

He listened for a minute, frowned, and said, "Why the hell don't you know? What kind of security officer are you?"

He paused while Bates explained what kind of security officer he was. "The army says the men are dressed in American fatigue clothes and they waved at the plane," the captain said. "How about that?"

I heard a hesitant murmur on the phone, then the captain said, breathing hard, "Camouflage? What the hell are you talking about?"

He put down the phone wearily, looked at us dejectedly, and walked slowly out. He never had much luck at the port office.

Pierce went out for dinner and then relieved me. "You may as well go down to the theater and get Woodley's girl," he said. "I'll send for you if I need you."

The Sweethearts on Parade turned out to be pretty much like the other USO units that had visited Adak. There were four girls and two men, one a balding master of ceremonies who sang "Mother Machree" in a thin falsetto. His humorous remarks depended entirely on sex, and it was a revealing characteristic of Aleutian life that everything he said aroused howls of laughter, spontaneous applause, and raucous guffaws.

The other man in the troupe was an old magician who went through the conventional routine of card tricks, disappearing handkerchiefs, and juggling balls. He was assisted by a seaman who had been "volunteered" for the job and handed the magician things when he asked for them. The audience showed little interest in the act but applauded at the end and made the magician take a bow.

The four sweethearts danced, individually and in chorus line, the two performances sometimes overlapping. The band made a moderate amount of noise, and when the acrobatic dancer did back-splits the audience howled. As long as they were on the stage, in gowns that revealed shoulders and suggested breasts, or appeared in the briefer costumes of acrobatic dancers, the men whistled, laughed, and shouted comments to the girls. The comments expressed, inelegantly but unmistakably, the speaker's opinion of the girl's shape or sexual potentiality, and disclosed his willingness to elaborate on these remarks in greater privacy and closer proximity.

On Adak, entertainers' talents had much less to do with their popularity than their sex did. Early in my Aleutian stay I had attended a performance by one of the world's greatest violinists, and he played extremely well that night. But the entertainment officer had booked him as only the first half of the evening's program, the remainder consisting of a western movie starring Tom Mix.

I went to the theater early to get a good seat, but there was no need to hurry. The crowd was no larger than usual. A sailor near me, who had come expecting only a movie, responded to the introduction of the violinist with some resentment.

"A fiddler," he remarked. "Can't say I care much for fiddlers."

When the violinist finished playing Bruch's *Concerto*, a marine near me said, "Say, Mac, that guy ain't bad. Why don't he play something we know?"

We heard next the "Flight of the Bumblebee." I turned to the marine.

"OK," he said, "the guy sure can fiddle fast. But I came here to see the movie!"

The demands for the movie grew louder, and the violinist relinquished the stage to Tom Mix. When I went backstage to tell him how much I had enjoyed the recital, he was very cordial, still wearing the cashmere sweatshirt and custom-made khaki trousers in which he had performed.

The Sweethearts on Parade were not exposed to any of the resentment that the violinist had faced, and the master of ceremonies announced that, in response to the insistent applause, the Sweethearts would introduce a "special" dance as an encore. "Boys," he said, "we're here to keep up your morale, and we got a number here that will really do it."

The special dance turned out to be an awkward exhibition of young women cavorting gracelessly on the stage. Bates, who was sitting next to me, applauded enthusiastically.

"Do you like that?" I asked.

"No," he said. "It's pretty damn bad."

"What are you clapping for?"

Bates grinned. "I want to keep up their morale. My God, think of working so hard at something they're so bad at."

I went backstage to get Eva. She looked considerably older than I had remembered her, and considerably tougher. While she was changing her make-up she asked what I thought of the show. I said it was fine.

"Glad you liked it," she bubbled. "Where's Pete?"

I explained about Woodley. A half-dozen officers piled into my jeep, each assuring Eva that hers was the best USO show he had seen and she was the best dancer in it. Eva did not object.

At the club everyone crowded around our table. The approaches varied from the aesthetic to the bawdy, but the purpose of all was the same.

"I live in Hollywood, Miss Jensen," Bates told her. "Do you know my friend Sam Goldwyn?"

Bates lived in Milwaukee and had kept his friendship with Goldwyn secret until that moment.

"You look tired, Miss Jensen," said Krueger. "I wonder if you'd care to rest in my room."

Eva smiled politely but her eyes kept roving. She poked me. "Who is that captain over there?"

I looked at the man who was leering at her from the bar. "That's Captain Bard," I said. "He's a character. He makes all his men get crew cuts."

"That's cute," Eva said. "He's bald as a billiard."

"He's about sixty, too," I said.

"He don't look that old," she said thoughtfully.

The steward came over and said I was wanted on the phone. It was Pierce. He said, "Woodley is dead."

I asked what had happened. He said that the crash boat hit a pinnacle and sank. The subchaser that was trailing saved all of the men except Woodley. By the time they had pulled him aboard he was unconscious, and he died before the ship got back to Adak.

I stood there for a minute, then hung up and went back to Eva. "I have some bad news for you," I said. "Peter has just been killed in an accident."

"Oh," she said, "ain't that a shame."

The men near us were quiet.

She took the glass Bates had been holding, tested it, and shook her head. "Too sour," she said. "I'm sorry about Pete. Ain't he the kid who told us he was saved by a miracle a couple of times?"

I nodded.

"Come here a minute," she said, pulling me by the sleeve. "I want to talk to you."

We walked over to the corner. "Why don't you introduce me to that Captain Bard?" she said. "It don't look like I got a date any more, does it?"

I turned and started to walk out. The steward reminded me about my coat, and while I waited, I looked back at Eva. Three men surrounded her, smiling and talking.

"What do you think of our base?" Bates said.

"It's swell," she giggled. "Lots of cute officers here."

"I have some Scotch at my quarters," Bates said. "Can I interest you in some Scotch?"

She giggled. I said, "Good night, Miss Jensen."

"Night," she said. "See you around."

As I walked past the bar, Captain Bard stood up and started toward Eva's section of the room. He had two drinks in his hand.

I drove down to the port office. The captain and Pierce and all our men were there. "Where is he?" I asked.

"In the hospital," Pierce said. "You can't see him now."

"How did it happen?" I asked.

"They hit an uncharted pinnacle. Dutton and Woodley were the last two in the water. They drifted apart. The sub-chaser got Dutton first, then went back for Woodley. It was too late.

"Just like that?" I asked.

"Just like that."

"Where is Dutton?"

"He's resting in his hut. He's all right."

I walked aimlessly around the room. The captain left, then Pierce. The rest of the men hung around, smoking and drinking coffee.

"Did they find the mystery boat?" I asked.

"Yeh," said Edwards. "It was four American soldiers on a fishing party."

"Then why—"

"Somebody forgot about them," Edwards said. "After we found them, the army remembered about the fishing party."

We sat around for a while and then Edwards said, "Well, we may as well go up to the hut. There's nothing we can do."

He was right. There was nothing we could do.

Chapter 15

At six o'clock on V-J Day when Buttaeus and I walked down, the salmon were still crowding each other and jumping out of the water in their relentless push upstream. The two seamen and their dog had gone, and on the shore lay the dead salmon they had dumped. We walked around the fish and got into the jeep.

"I'd better put in an appearance at the office," I said. "Can I drop you at the club?"

"If you don't mind," Buttaeus said, "I'd like to see the office."

The fog hung a few feet over the top of the jeep, and Buttaeus looked at it morosely. "Is that drab gray canopy always here?"

I smiled wryly. "The fog? I'm so accustomed to it I don't notice it any more." I drove on, slowing at a sharp mountain curve. "If you think this is bad you should see Adak in winter. When the williwaw blows, you have to shuffle slowly through the snow, leaning into the wind and holding onto Quonset huts to keep from being blown over. That bay is quiet now, but I've seen black waves, twenty feet high and more, crash violently against the docks."

The road straightened out as we approached the port building, and I relaxed at the wheel. "But it's not always like that. Sometimes there is a clear day and you can enjoy the rugged, rough beauty of the island. There is no flat land here—anywhere—only hills and mountains and sloping tundra. And on days like that you can see the smoking volcano on the next island, thirty miles away. You can see it clear and sharp, smoking steadily."

Pierce welcomed Buttaeus and introduced him to Dutton. Buttaeus sat down behind Woodley's desk and looked out into the bay. A Liberty ship was discharging cargo at the dock. Three small motor launches scooted around. Beyond the net, the patrol vessel passed, turned, and passed again. At four o'clock the minesweepers had sent in a message, asking whether they had to continue sweeping.

The commander thought for a minute, then asked Dutton his opinion.

"It's only four o'clock. They're supposed to work until five."

"Right," the commander said. "Tell them to continue sweeping. But if it's four o'clock, I'd better go over for some coffee."

A little later, Bates came in and sat down. "Yes, sir," Bates said, "it's all over. A year from now you won't remember there's been a war."

I smiled. "Remember that clipping you once showed us that called you 'Fighting Dan'? You never did get to see a Jap, did you?"

"Hell," said Bates, "I know what they look like. I've seen pictures of them."

"What are you going to tell your kids, Mr. Bates?" Nooters asked.

"Well," Bates said, "I guess you can't call this a picnic. I guess we've been in danger of attack up here all the time. Hell, I've got a man conducting gas-mask drills right now."

The navy had been on the island for three years and now, at the end of the war, Bates had organized compulsory gas drill. Nooters said, "Hey, I'm supposed to go through that gas chamber Saturday. You going to call it off, ain't you, Mr. Bates?"

"The hell I am. I don't call anything off till I've got orders. Hell, the army's got their men digging ditches today. You don't see them calling anything off, do you?"

"They'll get around to it," Nooters said.

"No they won't. What would those men do all day if we didn't make jobs for them? Hell no. Keep them working, I say."

Nooters puffed on his corncob pipe. "Mr. Ward, how soon do we get out?"

I said that the navy would soon publish its discharge system, giving points for length of service, overseas duty, perhaps wives and children. Nooters sipped his coffee thoughtfully.

"When I'm out, there ain't nothing to keep me from taking a poke at another civilian, is there?"

Bates laughed. "Nothing but the law, Mac."

Nooters took a long puff on his pipe. "When will the commander get out?" he asked.

"He is thinking of staying in," I said. "The personnel bureau is urging officers to apply for the regular navy."

"God damn," Nooters said. He pulled at his pipe, puffed for a while dejectedly, then brightened.

"Dutton ain't going to stay in the navy, is he?"

"Hell no," Bates said. "Dutton's getting out just as fast as he can."

"Six months, you think?" Nooters asked eagerly.

"Less than that," Bates said.

Nooters leaned back and puffed contentedly. When the coffee was ready, he poured it and brought cups to us.

"Have you heard from Manley?" I asked.

"I ain't, but the guy in his hut got a letter."

"Well?"

"I guess it worked out OK. He says his wife's back with him. He says she was just lonesome is all."

"He's got Woodley to thank," I said.

"Aw, bull," Bates said. "Before he's through, he may have Woodley to blame. Now I'll tell you a funny one I heard from Saunders today. A guy came in to see him 'cause his wife's running around. He wants her allotment stopped but he doesn't want a divorce. How about that?"

"What's funny about that?" Nooters asked. "I don't see nothing funny."

"O hell," Bates said. "You're just stupid."

Nooters scampered into the ship-plot room and a moment later the commander came in, smoking a cigar. "I've been in the captain's office," he said. "Big party at the club tonight. And free beer for the enlisted men at the recreation hall. The captain wants everybody to celebrate."

"I was thinking," Bates said, "for the regular navy this is the end of the damn road. A lot of those boys will be demoted to their permanent rank. How many of those bastards are really sorry it's over?"

"War is a seasonal business," Buttaeus said. "How do you feel about it, commander?"

Pierce hesitated. "I'll be frank with you," he finally said. "I'm surprised. Just one month ago the admiral called a meeting of all the officers on the base. His intelligence officer told us how long he expected the war to last. Twelve to eighteen months, he said. Right?"

Bates nodded. Pierce went on. "Well, when the admiral's intelligence officer gives you figures like that, you certainly pay attention. You make your plans on that basis. Now here it is, one month later, and the war is over. I'll tell you, it's disconcerting." Pierce put his cigar out and threw it into the wastebasket. "How about you, Jack? How do you feel about it?"

I looked up sheepishly. "I'm awfully glad it's over, and all I want is to get home. But I was just remembering that three years ago, before I went into the navy, I had visualized myself on the bridge of a cruiser, peering into the night, suddenly calling out vigorous commands to men who materialized around me. The details were confused, but they included a sudden change in course, the white wake of a torpedo just missing us, and a noisy outburst of anti-aircraft. Now I was thinking about this desk where I've been sitting for two years. It looks just like the desk in Chicago where I sat before the war. My civilian desk had one phone on it; this one has two.

"It's a depressing observation at the end of the war, and I'm sort of sorry I haven't read this war novel on my desk." I held up a book. "The critics all said it was a realistic picture of the war, and I took it out of the Red Cross library a couple of weeks ago so I could find out something about the war. But I never did get around to reading it, and now it looks as if I never will."

"Don't worry about it," Buttaeus said. "The critics don't know any more about the reality of war than you do."

"Hell yes," Bates bellowed, "those critics don't know anything. Don't worry about it."

"Thanks, Bates," I said gravely. "I won't."

The commander looked at his watch. "It's five o'clock," he said. "I think we can go now." He put away his papers and bent to tie his shoelace. "Damn," he said. "A knot." He tried to untie it, swore, then took a long knife out of his desk and cut the lace. He looked at the knife and smiled before he put it back. "You know," he said, "my wife gave me this knife when I went overseas. The ad claimed it's awfully handy when you're abandoning ship. I wouldn't know. I never used it before today, except once. That was to cut a candy bar." He closed the drawer and stood up.

"Anyone want a ride to the club?" he asked.

"No, thanks," I said. "I've got the jeep."

The commander and Bates left. I looked out the window for a long time. When I turned back, Buttaeus asked, "Do you mind my asking what you were thinking about?"

"Odds and ends. I was thinking that the word 'old' will never mean simply 'aged' to me. 'Old' in the navy applies to too many things: 'the old man,' describing the twenty-two-year-old captain of a small ship; 'old bastard,' characterizing a chief petty officer, 'old Jimmy,' referring to a seventeen-year-old seaman. I thought that in next month's roster I can write what I've long wanted to write: in the last column, 'duties in training for,' I will now write 'civilian.'"

"I thought of the man in a photograph I sent home. King and I had been standing in front of our hut, posing for a photograph. A drunken lieutenant who was walking by came over, pushed in between us, and put his arms around our necks. We tried to get rid of him but couldn't, so we went ahead with the photo taking. He shook hands with us affectionately and staggered off down the road. I had never seen him before and I never saw him again. I thought of him now, for a brief moment.

"I thought of the submarine scare a year ago, when all the planes went up and zoomed around and dropped bombs, and we had an alert of sixteen straight hours. They killed a small whale. I thought that the time President Roosevelt spent here on his visit was just about right for Aleutian duty: forty hours. I thought of the over-staffing up here, and the months wasted waiting, and pausing on Saturdays to listen to football games. I thought that incompetent officers keep referring to their civilian jobs, and incompetent men keep saying it's more important to be good than to be smart. And how the group focuses its hatred on some one man and blames him for everything and resents the nonconformist even when he is working for them. I thought of the gentle courage of the homely nurse whom one of the officers fell in love with and asked to marry. She told him to wait until they were back in the States; if, after seeing attractive women for a while, he still wanted to marry her, she'd be glad to be his wife. And I thought of King's description of naval reserves: 'reluctant warriors,' he called us."

I put away my papers and led Buttaeus down the hall. We stopped in front of the big bulletin board outside the executive officer's room. Under the permanent sign, "Motto of the Day," was a typewritten slip of paper. It said, "Early to bed, early to rise, makes a man healthy, wealthy, and wise." Buttaeus looked at the sign and shook his head; then we went out to the jeep.

When we arrived at the officers' barracks, Bates was shouting in the wardroom. "If that don't beat all. Blue uniforms. How about that!"

I asked what he was talking about. "Blue uniforms—regulation blues—somebody says that's the new rule. Here, on Adak, where there's more mud than anywhere else in the world. Hell, you can't step outside without getting into mud. We've gone through the whole damn war in old clothes and high shoes, and now they're going to make blue the uniform of the day, like that goddamn Englishman in the tropics who dressed for dinner."

Ensign Edwards came over, was introduced to Buttaeus, and said to me, "You'll be getting home soon, I guess."

"In a month, I hope."

"I've been here twelve months," Edwards said. "do you think they'll make me stay twelve more?"

I didn't know.

"I hope not," Edwards said. "There's going to be an awful lot of chickenshit here. Did you hear the scuttlebutt about the blue uniforms?

Next thing you know they'll be having daily inspections."

"It'll take a while to change. You applying for regular navy?"

"I don't know what to do. The captain's mad because Pierce is the only officer who applied. You know all those directives lately, urging young officers to stay in."

"Do you want to stay in?"

"No, but if I put in an application maybe they'll give me better duty until my time is up. Then I can change my mind."

"All right." I looked at Edwards closely. "But what's bothering you?"

Edwards motioned to the radio. "It's those damn programs. You know, Mr. Buttaeus, we usually listen to Radio Adak. It plays transcriptions of the better stateside programs, and it deletes all commercials. But today, since it's V-J day, they're tuned in to the States, and the crap I've been hearing makes me sick."

Edwards turned up the volume and we listened for a while. Then I said, "OK, I get the idea. Turn it off."

Edwards turned the radio off and scowled. "Here we are, on a desolate island three thousand miles from home, listening to sweet-voiced announcers fight the battle of war bonds. And these damned news analysts who guessed wrong day after day smugly commenting on victory. And sanctimonious bastards who got rich during the war making speeches about noble sacrifices. It makes me sick.

"If you feel that way in a non-combat area," Buttaeus said, "how do you suppose the men who've done the actual fighting feel when they hear pep talks from civilians who never flinched, never suffered, never heard a shot fired?"

Edwards nodded. "Sure. It's even more disgusting for them. Here it is V-J day, and all you can hear on the stateside radio is syrupy-voiced women and delicate men hinting that the Allied victory was due in no small measure to manufacturers of cosmetics, cigarettes, and patent medicines. And the civilians themselves—you'd think they actually fought the war. They've seen so many war movies, read so many newspapers, magazines, and novels, and heard so many radio sketches about war, they feel they've shared the danger and misery. They're familiar with some war slang, and they know that soldiers sometimes gripe, but they've been guaranteed that in a crisis 'our boys' always come through. By now they've had so many of these second-hand experiences and identified themselves with actual and fictitious characters so intensely, that they're convinced they've been in the war. Almost. They've got just enough guilty conscious left to make them yell about these things instead of say them quietly."

The clock struck seven and I asked about dinner. Edwards said he had already eaten. Buttaeus and I walked over to the mess hall. It was empty, except for two men at the senior officers' table. Young Lt. (j. g.) Rogers was sitting there with Commander Pierce. He was wearing a new uniform, with shiny gold braid on the sleeves, and he was listening intently and nodding soberly when the commander paused. Sometimes he looked thoughtfully off into space, as if he were deliberating on problems more profound than those an ordinary junior-grade lieutenant might be expected to be concerned with.

After dinner we walked towards the barracks. I stopped by the jeep and held the door open. "Where now?" Buttaeus asked.

"The cemetery."

We got in and I drove off slowly, watching the grayness above the island darken and the waves churn against the buoys, black rocks, and docks. When we approached the north end of the island, I drove up the ski-slide road, parked, and pointed out the wooden barracks of Tenth Army, the Quonset huts of the navy, and the white cross on the navy chapel. In the distance, across the dull gray bay, the lights of the harbor entrance control post shone dimly. There was no moon and there were no stars and there were no trees.

As we drove on, up the narrow, badly kept road, lights began to appear in huts and barracks. We were not far from the base, and the jeep bounced slowly along the road on the side of the mountain. I stopped when we reached a plateau, and we looked at the tundra in the shadows.

"What's that sound?" Buttaeus asked.

We listened. Very indistinctly we could hear a voice. "Let's see," I said, and we got out of the jeep and walked around the bend. About five hundred yards away, off the road, a light shone. We walked toward it.

"It's an army outpost," I said. "Four soldiers. They rotate them once a month."

The sound grew louder as we approached. "It's a radio," Buttaeus said. "They're listening to a broadcast from the States. Well, it's nice these poor guys can keep in touch with civiliza—"

He broke off when the announcer stopped talking. We listened for a moment to a twangy, grating rendition of a hillbilly tune, then turned and walked back to the jeep.

"Tell me," Buttaeus said quietly as the car wound slowly up the hill, "what have you learned in the war?"

I took a long time before I answered. "Not much. I had thought that in war I would experience and observe profound emotions. In the presence of imminent death I expected to see fear and courage and terror and greatness. Instead the perpetual tedium in the Aleutians merely intensified petty irritations, exasperating minutiae, and absurd exaggerations of minor infractions. On Okinawa and Iwo Jima and in Normandy people were dying, while the authorities on Adak complained about the listlessness of salutes and the width of the margins in official letters. I re-learned platitudes, that the weak are more cruel than the strong, that men find scapegoats to account for their own failure, that we are confused and ill informed and insecure. But I didn't need three years in the service to learn that or to learn that most men some of the time, and some men most of the time, are generous, kind, and brave. I remember what Woodley did for Manley and how he treated Telford. And I suspect that the rescue of Peter Woodley from an overturned canoe and a burning school and a crashed plane wasn't wasted."

Buttaeus looked straight ahead, and his voice was slightly hoarse. "It's wasted, all right," he said, "as far as any consolation is concerned. It isn't wasted, in the obvious sense that nothing that ever happens is really wasted."

"I tried to offer consolation to Woodley's mother, but I couldn't write a very convincing letter," I said.

"Is she a religious woman?"

"Yes."

"Then it shouldn't have been hard to convince her. All you have to tell people like her is that Woodley's death is proof of God's wisdom and love."

"I don't quite follow."

"It's simple enough." Buttaeus said, still looking straight ahead. "His mother is devastated by his death, but she is also disappointed because Woodley died before he did anything that human minds regard as important—like becoming a famous inventor, or financier, or statesman. Because in a business civilization people put aside objects for use in the future, they think that God too is operating a business and figuring profits and losses. You can tell Woodley's mother that God works on a higher level than that, and His saving an ordinary boy like Woodley is proof of his wisdom. If only great inventors, statesmen, or financiers were saved, what could the average human being hope for? If God's mercy was reserved only for the leaders of men, then the masses of men would be forsaken. No, it is precisely because Woodley died before he achieved conventional distinction that his mother can be comforted. It isn't the religious person whom you can't console."

At the cemetery the radio could no longer be heard, and our steps made squishy sounds as we walked among the graves in the dusk. It was very still and very remote.

There were not many graves in the Adak cemetery. Here lay a soldier who had died, according to official records, from food poisoning. Here was a marine who had been killed by another marine, a guard who came off watch one night, loaded his machine gun, and sprayed the barracks. By the time they knocked him out he had killed one man and wounded eight. The doctor explained later that the crazy marine had fought at Guadalcanal. He had been sent to the Aleutians for a tour of easy duty.

Two of the graves contained Japs. They had been captured on Attu and had been in the brig at Adak, awaiting shipment to the States, when they died. Some said they had killed themselves; some said they had failed to recover from wounds; one man claimed they had been shot informally. I didn't know.

These were the only Japanese on the island, but the marines on guard duty were still marching around the ammunition depot and the nurses' quarters. Woodley's grave was a few feet beyond the Japs', and it did not look fresh any more under the fast-growing vegetation. A mound of earth, a brownish green growth, and a few yellow flowers were lit up by the Jeep's headlights. The bouquet that someone had left leaning against the wooden cross had slipped and rotted. The cross itself was rotting in the permanent dampness of the Aleutians.

"Woodley would have been twenty-five next month," I said.

"My son will never be twenty-five either," Buttaeus said.

It matters to him, I thought, and it matters to me, but no one else cares, and soon I won't think much about it either. I'll be back in the States, enjoying the things Peter mentioned when we watched the salmon run, and I'll soon forget these monotonous months. They'll telescope into one gray blur, and the days will run into each other, in retrospect, with only a few high spots standing clear. It's not likely that anyone will visit the graves again. People make tours of cemeteries in Europe, in the Philippines, in Hawaii. There won't be many tours to the Aleutians.

We rode down the mountainside. Soon the williwaw would blow again and the snowline on the mountain would begin crawling down, and the clouds would begin to press heavy and low on the island. The two dead Japanese would be there, and the murdered marine, and the boy who died of food poisoning, and Peter Woodley.

Dr. Leonard Feinberg is Distinguished Professor Emeritus of English at Iowa State University. He taught courses in American literature, creative writing, and satire. Internationally respected as an authority on humor and satire, he is the author of a number of books including *The Satirist, Introduction to Satire, Asian Laughter, The Secret of Humor, Hypocrisy: Don't Leave Home Without It,* and *The ET Visitor's Guide to the U. S. A.*

Where the Williwaw Blows is based on Dr. Feinberg's two-year stint (1944-45) as a naval officer on the island of Adak in the Aleutians. In this darkly humorous novel, Feinberg turns a sardonic eye on the foibles of military life while he memorializes the quiet heroism of some of the men who were stationed on one of the bleakest military outposts of World War II.

Printed in the United States
901100004B